I0618470

Mass Incarnate

Dante D Gazzaniga

Book 1

ISBN-13: 978-0-9994440-0-9
ISBN-10: 0-9994440-0-X

Mass Incarnate

This book is dedicated to my love, Sierra L. Gazzaniga for putting up with me and all my fault and for losing your $1000 cat, Dr. Cornelius Waffles Doomclaw. We love you Waffles... Please come home. I love you with all my heart Sierra, and I am sure Waffles is just fine. I hope...

Mass Incarnate

CHAPTER 1

"The Unworthy"

"Make no mistake! There are two types of people in
   this world. Those that are victorious… and dead
   people."
                  Drill Sergeant Dante D. Gazzaniga

       In an alley in the middle of some big city, two
voices spoke just in the shadows as they gazed upon a
busy, crowded street. Dark and repulsed were these
voices.
       "The world and its populace have become…
unworthy. Useless murder, rape, and torment for
some… blind ignorance and an overly exaggerated
sense of privilege with others. Putrid… weak…" The
figure brought up an Insignia cigarette to his weathered
lips and dragged hard off its bite.
       "Humans have a life but don't know how to
live. Perfectly tuned bodies created for brilliance, yet
they live a pathetically dull existence. Mediocre! Most
will die off, and the memory of them will fade away in a
few years and then… forever. Why? They celebrated
ordinary like it's a god. Where are the dauntless and
the gallant-hearted? The artist and architects! The
great leaders! There's like a handful left, and even they
are not at their potential. Everyone else scurried for
that magic pill. They do not know struggle and

3

suffering." The other mocked waving off with his hand as he turned away.

"Vain they are. With no reason to be vain. Weak… Cowardly… Ignorant. They bicker over nothing. Victims! Victims to their Euphemism Treadmill. Scared… Desperately trying to be something they are not because they are unwilling to work for it. Billions died and left no mark on this… rock. All those lives… wasted! Pathetic these Humans have become… Unworthy of the life they have been bestowed. Inundation is required." The first figure drew off his cigarette again staring at the ground thinking deeply.

"We tried that once. No no no…. this time they will fight for it! It will be bloody!" the first figure said.

"Ha! They will not make it!" the second ridiculed.

"They will. Very few but they will. And I'm sure we will have a few surprises as well. They will learn from this lesson and us… it will teach it. Sink or swim or they will die off as a race. Either way, I don't care."

"Nosoi? Ragnarok?"

"Incarnation!" The second figure stated with conviction.

There was a long and awkward paused in the conversation. As time passed, the first figure seemed to become more and more agitated. Showing some stress in his action, he exhaled the smoke from within his lungs forcefully and flicked his cigarette with an angry jerk.

"Us? Or them…!?" he enquired, as he faced the first figure.

"Them of course! We can blame it all on her. She pierced the veil once. We'll just make it happen the same way again. They will all blame her for letting that filth out, and I know exactly who will help. He hates her more than anyone."

"Perfect..." the first figure whispered softly and much calmer now.

Just then a chubby angry little man stopped at the far end of the alley on the street side. He was talking into his cell phone to someone at his work complaining about whatever when he took a sip of his coffee. He grunted suddenly and quickly removed the paper cup from his lips as if it was diseased. In doing so, he had inadvertently captured the attention of the ominous figures as well.

"God damn it! They put regular creamer instead of French vanilla in my coffee! Damnit! Now my day is ruined!" He whined loudly like an overgrown child almost stomping his foot as he continued complaining about everything wrong in his life.

The first figure raised his stout war-torn hand slowly to his face and placed another cigarette on his lips. He then retrieved an exquisite and intricately engraved lighter from his pocket. Emotionless he held it up to the end of his cigarette and flicked the ignitor once. Blue and purple sparks erupted from its mantle but no flame. Pausing, he then glared at the little man as if he had seen a sickening act. A penetrating stare as if he was looking straight at the disgruntled little man's soul. He flicked the igniter again. This time, a brilliant blue flame arose from the lighter as he proceeded to lite his cigarette. The tobacco cracked at the flame as the figure pulled a long drag of smoke deep into his lungs. At the same time the little man, still complaining to whoever on the phone, burst into flames. Puzzled the little man just stood there and looked all around himself as if he was a kindergartener told to solve a physics equation. Then came the pain. Pain like he had never felt before or could have even imagined possible. His body is unscarred. Never knowing what it is to be injured. He began to scream hysterically taking in deep breaths pulling in gusts of flame. His every breath scorching his throat and lungs making each scream more... gurgly.

His body, lacking the ability to defend itself because it never had to, just hopped in one place flailing its arms about like a crazy monkey. And with all this drama nobody came to his aid. People on the streets gawked in horror while filming the event with their cell phones and some even ran around him and continued on their way. But nobody stopped to help. He soon dropped to his knees as the gurgling turned into an obstruction caused by burnt flesh and blood. His fate is now sealed. Moments later his body laid motionless on the sidewalk.

The two figures turned around and walked deeper into the alley. The first figure, a few steps in, turned his head slightly to the rear and said.

"Now your day is ruined." and pulled another drag of his smoke.

CHAPTER 2
"FML"

Lilith never knew where she came from or who her birth parents were. Her appearance was a complete mystery to everyone. The locals delivered her to Marcus and Abie Paean, who were a husband and wife Doctors. They dedicated their lives to providing medical care to the impoverished and war-torn country of Africa and its people for some time. And everyone else in the world that would let them care for them. Some hunters found her in a field naked and alone. It was apparently obvious she didn't belong there. The baby had blazing red hair, pale skin, and fat like a ham roast. Most children in Africa were malnourished and well... Dark skinned and definitely did not have red hair. The locals, confused, took her to the only white people they knew and of course, Marcus and Abie had no problem raising her as their own.

Her adventures as she grew were immense and highly unusual for a child's life. Lilith traveled around the world with the Paean's and lived very well. Lilith led a storybook life all the way up till she was 16. All that stopped tragically, and she evolved into who she is today.

At 27 years old Lilith stood an ample 5 feet 7 and wielded a truly unique athletic physic. A physique slaved over since she was a kid. Her body was carved out by discipline and hard work. No average man could hold a light to her strength and prowess. Her skin was porcelain and lightly freckle, her hair blazed as red as fire with eyes as green as Scottish Tufed grass.

Lilith prided herself on being fiercely independent. She would rather learn a skill then ask for help. At times, her independence intimidated people and scared some away. She usually scared most men off before the first date was over. But Lilith didn't care. She was alone… Not lonely. And euphoric that way.

Although her looks could be deceiving, she was more than just beautiful. She possessed something very few people in the world had. A Warrior's spirit, a competitiveness beyond approach, an inability to give up, and a ravenous need for to jump into any chaotic situation she could find. But most of all she needed to challenged and pushed outside her comfort zone. Living outside her comfort zone made her feel like she was alive. Lilith loved lazy Tuesday morning and relished them when they came. But her heart would always push her out into the world. Always the adventurer and always riding the blade. Because right there is where the magic happens, and she knew it.

Some people will never know the quiet of the Alaskan plains without hovering just over hypothermia in the middle of nowhere or even how huge the sky can get there. They will never know the feeling of isolation and desolation without having been washed overboard in a storm in the middle of the Atlantic or the pure elation of a glory after a decisive victory over your enemies. When you push the envelope both spiritually, mentally and physically, it is then that you find these little moments. Outside of your comfort zone and not on the couch. Definitely not in a cubical either.

She never really knew what the organization was that she worked for other than it was attached to the US government and that it was very hush hush. They titled her an Operative in the Army. However, she never enlisted. The organization attached her to Special Forces ODA 458 as an advisor. She didn't mind, though. They took her in when she needed a friend and took care of her.

Joey, her mentor, and ODA team leader pulled her in when she was about 16 and taught her everything he knows. When she was old enough, she then went to several military schools and foreign combat schools as if it was her hobby. French foreign legion, SFAS, Buds, PJ, British SAS schools, GSG9 training in Germany, and after learning enough Russian Lilith graduated as a Russian Spetsnaz foreign exchange student. She learned quickly... freaky quick. As far as she was concerned, Joey saved her life, and she was very thankful. She would often try to outdo Joe or at least impress him. She impressed him often enough. But he always seemed to come out on top somehow. But she was getting better every day. Joe knew it as well.

They carried a very professional leader-subordinate relationship that worked very well. All in all, Joe and Lilith considered each other family. They never addressed it of course. It was just one of those unspoken conversations that ended quickly with an awkward topic change.

She didn't know what drove her intensity, just that it was deep within her and constantly kept her competitive. All she wanted to do is destroy evil things. Drug dealers, Sex Slave Traders, terrorist, and tyrants. She wanted to kill them all and anyone that helped them. Her mind was always preoccupied with her next victory... and her next celebration. She did love a good party!

Magic and adventure filled her childhood. She learned how to hunt tigers in South Africa by tribal chiefs, learned how to play darts from Pilipino Pirates and chess with Irish Revolutionaries. All of them introduced to her during her travels with her parents.

But during these times, she also saw all the suffering that took place around the world. She became convinced that bad things happen to good people for no reason. All the tragedies people suffered because of the ignorance of others. She always mused...*how is it that the world loses their minds when a celebrity overdoses but doesn't bat an eye when millions of women in Africa are raped, mutilated and murdered every year?*

She swore to herself that this would end, and nobody will have to suffer like that anymore. She is always calm, but she is always filled with oceans of rage and vengeance. Our story begins.

South Africa – two weeks ago.

"Colonel . . . Five minutes!" The crewmen shouted.

"Right!" Lilith returned while inspecting the straps fastening her truck to the sled. She knew everyone was staring at her.

And Colonel...? What the hell was that about? She thought to herself fighting back a smile. Lilith knew Joe had something to do it.

Lilith is no stranger to people glaring at her. Just being a woman in a man's world is enough to draw looks. And given the situation that she is in now tips the scales to just plain strange. Some chick wonders up with a group of high-ranking officers telling you to get airborne in your pretty little C-17 cargo plane. F-22 Raptors appear out of nowhere as escorts. You might also want to know where it is you're going, but never asked because you were afraid to know. Although the crewmen were professionals, their constant looks and the fact that they were fumbling about like drunken apes were getting on Lilith's nerves. She finally ordered them to go away and let her finish the checks. She couldn't blame them. This whole situation probably looks crazy from all angles.

After completing her checks, she turned to the crew. Caught off guard, they abruptly and awkwardly turned away trying desperately to look busy. Lilith rolled her eyes and pulled her hair back into a ponytail. As she did, she remembered she still had makeup on from her date just hours before. Joes Idea... not one of his best.

The timing couldn't be more perfect. Now somewhat embarrassed Lilith shook off the feeling and reminded herself that something more important is in front of her. Makeup on or not she would probably never see these guys again anyway.

"Whatever! I wasn't having fun. That guy was such a jerk!" She thought reflecting on how great it was that she was able to leave and not hurt the guy's feelings too bad. She hated dating. It was so uncomfortable and repressive. It felt like she was trying to sell herself. What is she supposed to say? Oh yeah, last week I killed a Kango Warlord for the rape and dismembering of thousands of native women. I pulled his head off with a thirty thousand pound tow wrench while he was ratchet strapped to a tank. Oh, and I totally wrote it off as a "Freak Accident." LOL!

Suddenly Lilith's cell lit up and began ringing. She pulled it from her now empty tact bag and placed a small earpiece in her ear.

The crewmen turned and looked at the radio operator in amazement. They were thousands of feet up in in the air, cruising over hundreds of miles of open grassland. How the hell could she get a signal? The radio operator just looked back with an 'I don't know' look on his face.

"What am I doing here Joey?" Lilith asked into the mic smiling, somewhat amused at the crewmen's reaction.

"Lilith, sorry to bother you with this but you're the only one in range right now." Joey's voice sounded serious.

The whole team was on leave in various parts of the world, and Joe had an emergency mission he needed to be completed in a hurry.

"It's OK Joe. I needed some more chaos in my life!" Lilith stated.

Joey was a large man with a Greek god physique. His enormous stature towered over most. His eyes were kind, and he was very soft-spoken and polite. Adorning his 275 pounds of hardened bone and muscle Joe sported an increasable Grizzly Adams beard that was always well groomed. Although he comes off as a kind hearted well-mannered man to most; Lilith has seen this beast first hand. Not long ago she's seen him smash a man's skull with his bare hands, break bones like sticks and kill with an efficiency of a machine. Then an hour later he is barbecuing in a pair of Ranger shorts and flip flops, joking about midget strippers. He was meant to Operate.

"Let me get to the point." He started.

"Yes, please." She returned

"We have a suspected experimental virus problem at a local electrical plant in your area. It's being moved today to a nearby harbor for shipment to the US. Or so we believe. They should arrive in about an hour to the port for upload. Take it out there. This is purely a hit and run mission."

"What's the virus?" Lilith questioned.

"You don't want to know. Not only do you not want to know, but you also don't want to breathe it, touch it or be within 100 meters of it if it's exposed to the air. Life expectancy after exposure is about 30 seconds. It's extremely aggressive and tough. Fire will only spore the virus, so you'll have to destroy it with an anti-viral agent graciously supplied in your pack." Joey continued. "Oh! And for the good news... There is a cure! Unfortunately, it doesn't work as fast at the virus. Catch my drift." Joe stated sarcastically

"Wow! Maybe my date wasn't such an asshole after all." She returned. "Anything else?"

"Nope, that's about it. We will be tracking you by satellite. Everything else applies to ops outside the continental U.S.; you'll have to find your own way out if you miss your window. There's no support; all operatives are on mission or out of range. There's a resupply ten clicks out. It's already entered into your GPS." Joey finished.

"How do I ID the virus?"

"There's a convoy leaving the electrical plant as we speak, the virus is there somewhere. Identify the virus with a test kit in your pack, and then blow the lot. Cool?"

"Cool. See you soon!"

A red light inside the bay turned green, and Lilith quickly jumped in her truck. A super-modified Toyota Tundra Devolro Custom redesigned for military use. She strapped herself into a five point harness, turned to the Crew Chief with thumbs and secured her eye-pro. In the rearview mirror, she watched the ramp slowly open exposing the night air. Turning her attention back to her job Lilith flicked a few switches and attempted to start the motor. Cold starting the truck with all its modifications is always a problem. Lilith hit the start button, and the vehicle screamed a hideous noise like a large air tool stripping bolts. White smoke poured from the dual exhaust and out the back of the aircraft. Lilith quickly held up a hand signaling the crewmen not to pull the locks on the sled yet. The Crew Chief let up a little and waited. She sighed and tried again… and again and then a fourth time. Another crewman signaled her by waving his arms and then tapped his watch. Lilith ignored him and tried a fifth time. This time, the supercharged v-8 roared into life.

Lilith smiled and revved the motor over and over again. The throaty noise of the monstrous engine drowned out the sound of the C-17's four jets engines. The engines voracity was almost horrifying. The crew stood there stunned as the pilot called down trying to figure what went wrong. Now, giddy like a schoolgirl, Lilith gave the Crew Chief thumbs up and smiled.

The Crew Chief, shaking his head, started counting down from five on his finger so Lilith could see. When he reached zero, he pulled two levers and waved Lilith goodbye.

The C-17, now about 100 feet from the ground, powered up its engines and aggressively gaining altitude to help the sled out of the cargo bay. Three parachutes simultaneously deployed and began hauling the rig from the rear of the plane and into the open air. Lilith had a sense of free-fall for a few seconds until the sled made contact with the ground. Dirt and brush exploded about the truck as it violently came to a stop.

Reaching out the driver's side window, Lilith pulled a lever mounted to the sled. The lever triggered explosive bolts attaching the cargo straps to the truck as well as lowered the front ramp. She then hit play on her player and gripped the steering wheel. Looking through the windshield, she could see the C-17 disappears into a smoky haze of the night created by the hundreds of brush fires below. The sky was hazy with smoke illuminated by a full moon. The smoke reduced Lilith's visibility, but she didn't care. Moments like this are by far her favorite part of the trip.

Her truck housed a 500 cubic inch V-8 Motor, Supercharger with Nitrous Oxide. It produced upwards of 950 horsepower. Its tuned exhaust created a very throaty sound that gave Lilith goose bumps. She revved the motor for several seconds admiring the noise and readied herself.

"Too sweet!" She said under her breath.

Lilith flipped down a liquid crystal screen attached to her roll cage and turned on her GPS. She and her target locations quickly oriented themselves on the screen. Then, as the tribal like techno punk mix dropped the beat, she slammed the vehicle into gear launching it from the sled. The terrain was relatively flat. Brush fires burned most of the foliage making it possible to go 60 mph safely. Lilith opted more for cool 90 mph and was loving every mile of it.

About one kilometer from the harbor Lilith pulled the truck into a small ravine and covered it with camo net. The Camo-net made the vehicle relatively invisible in its surroundings or at least she hoped it did. She then grabbed her pack and weapons and jogged the rest of the way to the target area.

Checking her GPS, Lilith made it to the harbor in record time. Visibility was difficult in this area due to the darkness and the smoke from the fires. Nonetheless, Lilith used the limited visibility to her advantage and sneaked up to a berm just outside the harbor and the virus carrying convoy.

The convoy had already arrived ten minutes before and was in the process of loading its cargo onto a 300-foot freighter. There was only one platform truck in the convoy, the rest of the vehicles were made up of jeeps and a couple of specialized fast attack all-terrains. This thing was well protected Lilith thought to herself as she began plotting her assault.

She made her way to the front of the freighter undetected and boarded her by the bow lines. Peeking over the edge of the ship's bow Lilith could see two guards smoking cigarettes watching the brush fires through binoculars. Quietly she made her way behind them and down the deck to where she found an open cargo well. Two dock workers positioned the cargo container from the convoy as if was suspended from the freighters crane in the middle of the cargo bay. Scanning the area, Lilith was surprised that the convoy was so heavily guarded yet the freighter only had a handful of guards. Even more surprising Lilith saw that the guards on the ship looked as if they were preparing to leave.

Not stalling, Lilith found an access ladder to the cargo bay of the ship and quickly slid down it. Silently landing on the floor, she paused for a second to check her situation. Noticing nothing that would cause her concern Lilith moved into the bay. Making her way behind several tractors, she again re-checked her situation. The dock workers finally finished securing the cargo container to the deck of the freighter and were checking their locks. Once satisfied the container was secure they turned and walked across the bay exiting through a door on the opposite side. Audible clicks told Lilith they locked the door behind them. Lilith suddenly felt uncomfortable. Something felt wrong, and she didn't know what. That warm and fuzzy feeling she had once was now leaving.

This is too easy. What the hell... She thought. *No turning back now. Just get it done.* She thought to herself.

Joey had warned her about loosening that warm and fuzzy you get when everything is going good. Lilith had always demonstrated an exceptionally well focused and intuitive awareness of her surroundings. She has saved the lives of every member of her team more than once with her ability. Pulling them out of the path of sniper fire before the shot was even heard or stopping their convoy without warning feet away from a roadside bomb.

However, she had no real evidence right now proving she was in danger. Well, other than she was sneaking onto a freighter, heavenly guarded by armed henchmen and loaded with a very vicious virus. Other than that... things were peachy.

Pulling a small wad of plastic explosive from her vest, Lilith inserted a wireless detonator into it and bolted around the tractor. She then chucked the wad across the room. It landed near the locking mechanism of the door the dock workers left through. She then slid on her knees in front of the cargo container and pulled a small hand held cutting torch from her belt and cut the locks off. Quietly, she entered the container, drew a red and black Infinity 1911 from its holster and flicked on the weapons tactical light.

In the middle of the container, she found a small table bolted to the floor. Secured in a plastic case was a 9-inch long vented metal cylinder. Encased in the cylinder was a small glass tube containing a clear brownish liquid. Lilith quickly moved to the case and opened it. She then retrieved the cylinder from its cradle and pulled the anti-viral agent auto-injector from her pack. Lilith pressed a button on the side of the autoinjector, and a four-inch spike jetted out from one end. Carefully she aligned the auto-injector with the sealed port on the end of the cylinder and prepared to inject the anti-virus. Something was wrong, but she didn't know what yet.

Static burst through her ear piece and startled her. It was her COMlink. Although she was in a cargo container, her reception should still be good. Lilith then thought that maybe she was being jammed.

That can't be. Lilith thought to herself. *There's nothing high tech enough to jam our coms.*

Shrugging the thought off Lilith turned her attention to the task at hand and began to realign the auto-injector again.

More static came through her comlink again and then again. Her heart started to race; she moved her COMlink closer to the container door. The static appeared again, but this time, she heard a voice creep out of the white noise. Faint but clear enough. It was Joey.

"LILITH... TRAP....GET THE HELL OUT!"

She closed her eyes and could faintly hear a rifle being charged from on top of the cargo bay. Her heart froze. Retracting the auto-injector needle, Lilith threw both objects down her shirt and exploded out the door in a dead sprint. Gunfire erupted from above blasting through the thin layered cargo container obliterating it in moments.

The ambush was not just moderate weapons fire either; these guys were using heavy crew served weapons like M2 .50 caliber machine gun and M240Bs. Lilith then double tapped a relay on her earpiece and the exit door exploded in front of her tearing it from its hinges and launching the door across the bay. Bursting through the doorway and into a corridor more rounds impacted behind her.

Two men dressed in tactical gear and armed with AK 47's just down the hall desperately trying to regain their senses from the blast. While still in a full sprint Lilith drew a long double edged blade from a sheath attached to her shoulder and as if throwing a softball drove the blade deep into the upper abdomen of one man killing him instantly. Using her momentum, Lilith then kneed the other in the face just shy of crushing his skull and knocking him out cold. Standing over him, she drew her pistol from her hip holster and shot him in the head without even giving the act a second thought.

Noticing a ladder to her left Lilith grabbed one of the AK 47's and scurried quickly up it to a hatch. Surprise and confusion were still to her advantage but not for long, and she knew it.   Bursting from the hatch Lilith opened up with an onslaught of automatic gunfire into the ambushing squad sending several men leaping into the cargo bay and killing the rest.

"GET OFF THAT BOAT LILITH!" Joey shouted through the radio.

Lilith smirked a little and leaped from the hatch door sprinting down the deck to the bow. Two men came around the corner in front of her. Lilith fired twice dropping them in place. Realizing the AK was out of ammo she tossed the weapon to the side and drew her 45s from their holsters in one smooth motion.

Breathe and focus...

Leaping from over the edge of the railing, Lilith firing her pistols dropped four more guards before hitting the deck below. Two levels up, however, three more men were preparing two belt feed machine-guns and a mounted M2 machine gun. The thin sheet metal of the boat wouldn't protect her from the M2 rounds; she decided to jump ship.

Looking across the deck, Lilith found a rope attached to the bow of the boat and sprinted for it.

Holstering her pistols, she snatched up the rope and darted across the deck to the river side of the ship. With the line pulled tautly and at a dead sprint, she leaped overboard. The Crew served weapons opened fire with a thunderous assault, slamming rounds relentlessly into the deck. Wood, sparks, and metal splintered violently in all directions. But it was too late. Lilith was off the ship.

Swinging in a slow arch across the front of the boat, Lilith stayed just ahead of the gunfire, and just above the water's surface. As she ended her swinging arc towards the dockside, she let the rope go and launched herself into the air and onto the roof of a dock house nearby. Landing on her knees, she slid across the dockhouse roof as rounds impacted the building from all angles. Reaching the other side, Lilith bounded off the edge twisting around in the air and returned fire towards the boat.

Impacting the ground hard on her back she rolled protecting the virus as best she could. Quickly she leaped to her feet shaking off the hard impact with the ground. Lilith then raced for cover behind several tractors reloading her pistols on the way. As she skirted the tractor, two guards on a dirt bike rounded the corner firing pistols. Leaning to her left avoiding the fire Lilith then spun around and kicked one of the men off his bike. Without pause, she shot the man in the face, holstered her pistols and mounted the now riderless bike. Heading for open land, Lilith worked through the gears quickly.

As she left the dock area, she looked behind her and noticed dozens of men scurrying for the convoy vehicles preparing to give chase. Pushing the bikes max power range Lilith reached its top speed quickly and ran like hell.

After a few moments, Lilith let off the throttle a little and glanced behind her. Rage filled her mind. She didn't like losing.

She was more than a little mad. However, she wasn't crazy. At least that's what she thought. Two 45 calibers and a dirt bike had no chance against squad based fast attack vehicles with mounted M2 .50 Caliber Machine Guns with thermal and night vision as well. Lilith hit the throttle again and headed for the truck. Her truck, however, was a man-eating demon.

Joe's voice burst through the COMlink but was inaudible through the static.

"SAY AGAIN JOEY! YOU'RE UNREADABLE!" Lilith shouted into the mic.

"AIR WEAPONS TEAMS FROM THE EAST...6 MIKES OUT!" Joey shouted over the static.

Lilith swore to herself as she tried to juice a little more speed out of the bike.

"COME ON!" she growled loudly wrenching the throttle.

If I can only make it to my truck! She thought.

Several minutes later Lilith finally made it to the ravine where her truck was hidden. The Pursuing vehicles had just caught up with her and had already opened fire. The two specialized fast attack all-terrains had M2 .50 calibers and 40 mm grenade launchers mounted on their frames. They would pose the biggest problem Lilith thought as she propelled the bike into the ravine.

Fragmentation grenades impacted the far edge of bank throwing dust into the air. Lilith finally made it to her truck and leaped from the bike running before coming to a complete stop. She then tossed the camo net off the truck and jumped inside. The fast attack vehicles reached the raven and leaped across just over her head. Lilith hit the starter, but it only kicked over in a pathetic attempt to start.

"No No No! COME ON BABY!" She tried again.

Hitting the starter again white smoke began billowing out of the exhaust pipe giving her position away but to no avail. It still didn't start.

Thumping from the 40mm grenade launchers could be heard in the distance, and Lilith knew she had to move. If she bails from the truck, she would surely get captured. But if she can't get the truck started the 40mm grenade would make short work of her.

"FUCK! AAAAGH!" she screamed hitting the starter again. The engine cranked but slower this time. The battery was dying. As its massive pistons chugged intermittently, a dark cloud of inevitable doom fell over her.

Not now… not here! Her internal voice whispered in her head desperately.

Like a startled Fiend the truck suddenly eruption into life. Not wasting time comforting herself Lilith Slammed the truck into reverse and hammering the throttle. The wheels hurled dirt forward as the massive truck launched from the ravine just as two grenades impacted in front of her. Lilith J-turned the truck around and powered up the side of the canyon. She then launched the vehicle into the air slamming it hard on the top side. Pulling a switch on the shifter, she locked a magnetic pulley that engaged the massive supercharger mounted to the motor. At 5500 rpm's the supercharger screamed into life like a hungry beast. Lilith then began working through the gears and positioned herself to give chase.

The Fast attack vehicles were quick, and she knew they could outmaneuver her as well. Trying to stay on the offensive she flipped three safety switches which armed three huge NOS tanks mounted behind her.

Two Jeep Rubicon's finally caught up to the group as the fast attack vehicles tried to find a way back across the raven. All four vehicles began laying suppressive fire in Lilith's general direction. Several rounds impacted into the side of the truck and both front and rear windows shattered. With her vision obscured Lilith pulled her foot off the accelerator and kicked the front windshield out of its frame and off the vehicle. Wind blasted her face as she peered out and noticed two helicopters opening up 20-millimeter cannons into the ground just ahead of her.

"SHIT!" She shouted.

Pulling the wheel hard to the left to avoiding the cannon fire, Lilith slammed her foot on the accelerator. The two helicopters pulled hard banks in unison and came in behind her. Looking in her side mirror, Lilith noted that the fast attack vehicles had made it across the raven and were almost in firing range.

Slamming the truck into fourth gear, Lilith tapped the NOS button nervously.

"NOS armed." A deep electronic voice stated. That was one of Lilith's little add on's. It just sounded cool.

A red button on her shifter began to blink wildly. Slamming the vehicle into fifth gear, Lilith hit play on her sound system, and a Rob Zombie remix began to thump away. Once she felt the motor hit its powerband, she fired the NOS. As the music started to blast, the truck launch forward with incredible power, pushing Lilith into her seat. The electronic voice then counted down from five as Lilith drove her vehicle dangerously close to its rev limit. Once the NOS discontinued its assault on the motor, Lilith found herself was well above one hundred twenty miles per hour and safely out of cannon fire range, for now.

Several seconds passed, and Lilith arrived at more brush fires. Slipping her goggles down to help see through the smoke she then buckled in and got comfortable. Down shifting to about eighty-five mph, Lilith made a slow arch to her left and prepared her vehicle for combat. Pulling a small respirator from under her center console, she attached the device around her nose and mouth to protect her from the smoke. To her right, Lilith pulled a hydraulic lever and erected a twin mini-gun rig up and out of the windshield of the truck and locked into position on the passenger side of the cabin. Pulling another lever, she armed the guns and flipped a switch that started the barrels rotating at high revolution.

Flames, smoke, and sparks from the fires burst about her vehicle as she turned around. Speed kept her truck from catching fire as she made her way to her first target.

The four pursuers reluctantly entered the brush fires as the helicopters hovered above searching for a target. The smoke and fire made searching the area difficult, and with the continuously varying updrafts, the pilots of the helicopters had a difficult time staying on station. Everyone was focused, and the radio was silent for several minutes. It had seemed that she might have gotten away the pursuers hoped.

Unwillingly, the Team Leader decided to call off the search. He may not have been entirely convinced Lilith got away, but he did not like putting his ass on the line like he is either. Reaching for the radio mic, the Team Leader told the driver to turn around and head back to the port. When he did, he noticed the horror in his driver's eyes. Lilith had pulled in behind them. He shrieked into the mic inaudibly in an attempt to inform the others of Lilith's position as the driver nailed the throttle of the little Jeep. Although the Jeep made a tremendous effort to accelerate Lilith's supercharged motor was, and for lack of a better word, overkill. She slammed the iron brush guard into the rear end of the jeep with such force it almost knocked the driver and team leader unconscious. Lilith then poured hundreds of rounds into its rear window completely obliterating both the driver and the Team Leader. She felt a little better knowing she's now on the assault and not on the receiving end of the ambush.

Catching sight of one of the fast attack vehicles out of the corner of her eye and under cover of the smoke and flames Lilith jerked the wheel right and pulled up to her pursuers right. The vehicle and their Gunners were firing blindly into the open attempting to get a lucky hit. Lilith stayed in their blind spot and pulled a 40-millimeter grenade launcher from her center console. While steering with her knee, she loaded the weapon, aimed and fired.

The round smashed into the side of the vehicle producing a concussion blast flipping the vehicle over and tumbling it to a stop killing everyone on board.

Glancing forward, Lilith saw one of the Jeeps cross her gunsights. The vehicle had caught fire as the driver frantically tried to find his way out of the blaze. Lilith, just trying to help out, pulled the trigger on the mini-guns. Rounds impacted into the Jeep side shredding it and ruptured its tank. The vehicle exploded suddenly flipping it end over end. As she watched the vehicle disintegrate Lilith hit a small mound of dirt launching her truck into the air sending rounds wildly into the sky near missing the helicopters.

"Whoa! Fair enough then!" she stated trying to get control of the vehicle back.

Both pilots panicked taking evasive action at the unpredicted attack. The Pilots, feeling a little more exposed now, decided to team up and strafe fire the entire sector.

Searching the landscape for several moments, Lilith found the last pursuing vehicle and pulled in behind it about twenty meters back. Just as she did several rounds hit the truck and blasted the ground around her. One round shot through the cabin of the vehicle close to Lilith's leg, jerking it away instinctively as she cursed aloud.

Lilith heaved the wheel left and then suddenly right. 20 mm rounds impacted around the vehicle launching dirt and hot ash into the truck burning her face and arms.

"Fuck!" she yelled.

Warning lights then flashed on the dash warning that the vehicle was beginning to overheat. Glancing at the water pressure gauge, Lilith decided that the brush fire was taking its toll on the truck and hoped the helicopters didn't hit the cooling system... yet. She needed to get out of there quick.

The last vehicle was between her and the open landscape. She needed to work quickly. Lilith pulled the trigger to the miniguns, and they immediately burst into a vicious eruption of fire and noise. She could feel the recoil of each round hammer her entire organs.

Then suddenly and with a loud metallic ring, the weapons system ceased. Lilith tapped the trigger several times but to no avail. She was out of ammunition.

"Fuck!" Lilith, she shouted. She knew she would have to do this the hard way.

Downshifting, Lilith hit the gas, and the truck lurched forward with a roar. The driver's shotgun man saw Lilith through the smoke and fire coming in fast and began shouting into his mic.

"She's right behind us man! Go! GO!"

"Keep her busy! I'm going to draw her out into the open and let the choppers take care of her!" the driver shouted back

"Just fucking hurry man!"

Scrolling her GPS, Lilith located an airfield less than a few miles away and locked it in. Downshifting she began her run for the airport. Although, once she was out of the brush fire, she knew she would have to deal with the helicopter and prepared herself for a dirty fight.

The shotgun man popped the five point harness off, spun around in his seat and drew a pistol firing repetitively behind him trying to get Lilith off their ass. But his efforts were unsuccessful and only pissed her off.

Lilith hit the gas and rammed the smaller vehicle with enough force to push it out of the way. Shifting down, she blew by the vehicle as if it was standing still.

Jerking the wheel, Lilith pointed the truck to open land and punched the NOS. The weight of her body sank into her seat as the vehicle launch out of the burning brush. She made it a good 500 meters before one of the co-pilots notice the smoke and dust filled vapor trail she left behind. Both Pilots immediately maneuvered to give chase with the fast attack vehicle not far behind.

A mile into her run Lilith came under fire from the helicopters. Debris and dust burst around her truck as she attempted to evade their cannon fire. Her efforts, however, were mostly in vein with the amount of ammunition hailing down.

Fist-sized holes were being punched into the body of her truck as she desperately tried to protect its engine and transmission. She could feel the rounds impact the hull of the vehicle in her bones. Burning Sparks and shrapnel blasted the inside of the cabin as Lilith ducked as best she could trying to cover her face. She grunted aloud in protest the closer each round came.

Wiping the soot from her gauges, Lilith began to realize all the vehicles systems were failing. Black and white smoke billowed out from under the hood as the Helicopters ruthlessly hammered Lilith's truck. Saying a small prayer under her breath, she kicked on a second oil pump and hit her last shot of NOS. Slamming the truck into sixth gear, she made 130 mph before ramming through the fence line of the airport subsequently blowing the engine.

It all started with a shrieking sound that gained in volume and intensity. As if metal on metal parts began shearing apart slowly. Then suddenly there was an ear-piercing clang and then a deafening silence for a half a second. The motor had seized up hard and permanently.

Just as she hit the tarmac, Lilith heard another loud thud, and then the truck jerked up like a wrecking ball hit it. The transmission finally gave out as well and locked up in gear.

The vehicle began a four wheel neutral skid at almost 100 mph. Lilith frantically tried to keep it upright but was having a trying time as more rounds slammed into the rear bed of the truck blowing out the tires. The right rim then jammed into the road ripping the rear suspension off and flipping the truck onto its driver's side.

Sparks and debris flooded the inside of the cab as Lilith raised her arms to protect her face. The truck seemed to slide for miles before it finally came to rest three hundred meters past the fence line.

Grunting loud and taking a deep breath Lilith popped the quick release on her harness and rolled out the front windshield onto the tarmac.

"Fuck me right!" she yelled in protest.

Dizzy and a little disoriented she made it to her feet pulled an M-34 rifle and bandoleer from a cargo box attached to the front bumper of the truck and darted away.

More rounds impacted around her stopping her in her tracks. Instinctively Lilith dropped to the ground and covered her head as more cannon fire blasted past her just a few feet away. She was about to jump to her feet when the helicopters shot by her only feet off the ground and at full throttle. She needed cover and quick.

An old vintage cargo freight plane filled with weekend skydivers suddenly came to a stop two hundred meters away when they realized things were getting a little hot on the tarmac.

Although the scene was very bizarre, the pilots weren't genuinely concerned until the helicopters began blasting the airfield up with cannon fire.

"Oh shit!" the pilot yelled. "Drop the rear gate...! Get the fuck out' a here!"

The pilot and co-pilot then jumped into the cargo bay and ushered everyone out of the aircraft as quickly as they could.

"Run God damn it!" they yelled over and over as everyone scattered away.

Lilith, in direr need of cover, began sprinting the two hundred meter to the soon to be abandoned aircraft.

About half way to the plane the fast attack vehicle breached the fence line to her right at incredible speed. She knew she would never make the aircraft in time and immediately went prone. Raising the weapon level, Lilith took careful aim on the driver's head and squeezed off three rounds. Although she was on target, the rounds skipped off the bullet-resistant glass-hurling them harmlessly away.

The fast attack vehicles Gunner targeted Lilith as best he could with his thermal sights and laid suppressive fire with the mounted .50 caliber machine gun. The driver hit the gas and maneuvered to ram her.

Slow your thoughts...

Lilith lowered her weapon slightly and breathed in forcefully through her nose, closed her eyes and held her breath for a count of four. Rounds fragmented the tarmac around her blasting her in the face and body from all angles with tar and pebbles. And then with an audible grunt, she exhaled out her mouth and let all the stress follow.

Smoothly....

Now almost emotionless she opened her eyes to a swarm of red tracer rounds flying past her. As if time had slowed to a crawl Lilith raised her weapon and targeted the expose front suspension system.

Squeeze....

She let loose one round which pierced the upper steering support turning the left front tire inward with a jolt. At that speed, the resulting suspension failure instantly put the vehicle into a roll.

Lilith rolled out of the way as the fast attack vehicle tumbled past her just in a fire roll end over end. Not wasting time admiring the result of her efforts Lilith jumped to her feet and again sprinted to the cargo plane. The fast attack vehicle exploded, and Lilith knew that would blind the helicopters FLAR system temporarily and took advantage of the situation.

The cargo plane stood ready to receive her with engines running and ramp down. At a full sprint, Lilith grasped the ramps hydraulic system support and swung herself up and into the cargo planes bay. The two copters blasted by the Cargo Plane searching desperately for her. It didn't take long for the pilots to figure out Lilith must be in the aircraft below and quickly brought their guns on target.

Lilith, realizing that rounds would be entering the craft at any second, rushed to the pilot's seat and slammed the throttles forward hoping a moving target would be harder to hit.

The aircraft roared to life and lurched forward from the torque of the four powerful motors. Quickly jumping into the pilot's seat, Lilith checked the controls and prepared for flight.

Rounds began impacted the hull of the aircraft making a popcorn like sound. This type of aircraft depended on an entirely serviceable hydraulic system, and Lilith shuddered at the thought of one of the rounds severing a line. Again the helicopters passed overhead in a low swooping arc, but Lilith, fully committed on her advance down the runway, ignored them and pressed on.

Once she approached take off speed, she pulled up on the steering and launched the hulking aircraft in the sky as fast as it would go. The engines roared louder as she forced the throttles wide open. The plane shuddered violently under the stress of abrupt and extreme takeoff. Lilith knew that the helicopters wouldn't be able to go as high and as fast as the cargo plane could and attempted to gain as much altitude and speed as she could in as little time as possible. Unfortunately, the helicopters were a lot quicker and were able to fall in behind the hulking aircraft.

Lilith, looking around, suddenly lost that warm and fuzzy feeling again. She couldn't see the helicopter anymore and figured that they must be behind her. Quickly she rolled the aircraft to the right and pitched the nose down. The colossal aircraft leaned reluctantly at first then charged towards the ground gaining speed as it went. The pursuing helicopters tried in vain to shoot down the faster vehicle but were unable to maintain accurately fire at the same time. Several rounds struck the hull of the aircraft, but no serious damage resulted.

Static blasted into Lilith's ear piece as Joey attempted to make contact. Quickly gaining altitude again Lilith called back into her mic requesting Joey to repeat his last transmission. More static blasted and Lilith thought she heard Joey's voice in distress about something. The helicopters must have had a jamming device onboard Lilith thought. She knew that the further away she got from them the better her coms with Joey would be.

Leveling off at ten thousand feet Lilith initiated the autopilot, bolted from her seat and sprinted into the cargo bay of the aircraft.

She dropped to her knees and slid for about ten feet while quickly pulling out the virus filled tube and the anti-viral auto-injector from inside her vest. More crackling came from her earpiece, but she ignored it. She knew it was Joey's voice shouting about something unrecognizable. But this was her chance to get rid of the virus finally.

"Hold on big guy... I almost have it!" Lilith's yelled into the mic.

She raised her arms in front of her in an attempt to steady herself against the turbulence of the aircraft and released the auto injector's spike. With a loud audible click, it locked into place. She then slowly brought the two tubes together in front of her and carefully aligned them so she wouldn't accidentally stick herself.

Just as Lilith was about to inject the antiviral agent into the virus tube, she heard Joey over the mic. "AIR TO AIR COMING IN LOW AT YOUR EIGHT O'CLOCK! EVADE! EVADE!"

EVADE... time slowed as she glanced at the cockpit.

FUCK! She thought knowing full well she would never make it. Horror immersed her lungs like a thick smoke.

Out of instinct, Lilith turned and glanced to where her 8 o'clock would be if she were in the pilot's seat and for a fraction of a second she swore she could hear the missile approaching. She blinked in anticipation. Time still crept by agonizingly slow...

The side of the hull exploded knocking Lilith across the cargo bay, slamming her against the bulkhead. The impact shattered the virus tube and the clear brownish liquid splashed onto her face and chest. Debris and smoke swarmed the inside of the aircraft as Lilith realized she had just been infected and freaked. She spits the liquid out of her mouth in vain. The Spicy taste made her gag and cough.

"Fuck!" Lilith shouted in frustration.

Quickly she forced her way to the pilot seat pushing debris out of the way and fighting the blasting wind from the now 5-foot hole in the hull. In her head, she began counting her last seconds away remembering that she only had 30 seconds or so to live. Her final job was very clear now.

"1...2...3..."

Reaching the pilot seat coughing and gagging Lilith knew she had to dump the aircraft in a remote area so the virus wouldn't infect innocent citizens. Yelling in her mic hoping to be heard, Lilith gave a situation report.

"I'VE BEEN INFECTED! GOING TO DUMP AIRCRAFT ON THE SIDE OF THE MOUNTAIN! CALL IN CONTAINMENT, ASAP!"

"18...19...20..."

The aircraft shuddered under the new stress created by the hole in the hull, and Lilith found it difficult to maneuver. Placing the aircraft in a steep dive, she increased engine speed quickly to full power. Aiming for the frozen peak of a mountain range just a few miles away, Lilith desperately hoped the cold would contain the virus long enough for a containment team and clean up crews to arrive.

"21...22...23..."

Lilith began to feel nauseous but still didn't feel any effects from the virus yet. Her heart was pounding hard in her chest like artillery cannons going off. She began to catastrophize what the virus would do to her body, and it made her shudder in the pilot's seat.

Altitude warning lights and sirens began blasting as the aircraft desperately attempted to get her attention.

"30...31...32..."

Questions began racing through her mind. Was I immune? Was Joey wrong? Is this a trick?

What the...?

"33..."

Lilith then took a whiff of the liquid on her hand and couldn't believe what she recognized it to be...

"Whisky!!!... What the fuck!!!!"

By sheer reaction, Lilith jammed her feet into the dashboard of the plane pulled back on the rudder like a powerlifter pulling a weight off the ground. The sudden physical demand on the aircraft made it tremor so violently Lilith's entire body went numb with pain. She couldn't even take a reading from the altimeter. Everything began to blur.

"JOEY... SOMETHINGS WRONG!"

"What the hell is going on!?! Are you infected!?!" Joey's voice emerged through the static and engine noise.

"I'M GREEN...! I'M GOOD...! SORT OF!"

The top of the mountain came up quick as Lilith struggled desperately to gain altitude. Metal could be heard shearing off of its supports and rivets popping from the stress.

Sweat, dust, and soot poured down her face making it difficult for her to see. The nose of the aircraft inched its way up as Lilith began to feel the panic well up inside her like a volcano about to burst. Can she get the nose up in time, will the aircraft break apart under the stress and damaged it has suffered, or will her pursuers shoot her down before she has a chance to do either.

"MOTHER FUCKER!!!!" Lilith growled under her breath and gritting her teeth. Two Hellfire missiles trailed past the craft and slammed into the mountainside throwing debris and snow against the haul. The question of her pursuers seemed to have answered itself, and she knew that even if she were able to get past the mountain side, the pilots would not have a hard time targeting her. Once she was safe from the crash, she knew she had to bail and bail fast. The lumbering aircraft was no match for fighter aircraft of any kind.

Wrapping her legs around the rudder to hold it still Lilith pulled two flexicuffs from her plate carrier's inner compartment and secured the rudder to a metal support just behind her seat.

The cargo plane shuddered violently under the turbulence and the G forces of the maneuver Lilith put in, and she had a tough time making her way to the rear of the plane. Lilith heard a loud crack and assumed the structural integrity of the aircraft was beginning to fail. Rivets from the inner hull exploded from their seat and shot across the cockpit busting out the windshield and slamming into Lilith's side. Pain seared up Lilith's side as she covered her face and rolled the rest of the way off the seat. G-forces propelled Lilith to the back of the cockpit and slammed her against the cockpit door knocking the wind out of her. Frantically trying to catch her breath Lilith managed to open the door grunting from the pain and the weight.

Wind and debris blasted around her making her task even more difficult to move. Making matters worse she realized in an immensely violent way that she had reached the mountain top.

The aircraft launched itself off the top of the mountain dragging its belly across its summit. The jolt of the impact ricocheted through the hull of the vessel heaving Lilith backward through the cockpit door. Grasping the edge of an open storage locker, she grunted with astonishment at the sudden jolt. With her feet dangling into the cargo bay Lilith looked over her shoulder. A large rift in the hull made up of about twenty feet of jagged metal had formed as a result of the missile attack. The aircraft was breaking apart, and she had to do something now, or she was going down with it.

"Fuck!" she shouted in protest.

The support beam that Lilith used to secure the rudder controls finally gave way and released its tension. The aircraft wavered a bit and then righted itself at full vertical. Lilith knew things were not looking good for her situation. Fire alarms sounded in all four engines. If she didn't think of something soon, the aircraft will either stall in midair, break apart or burn up. "FUCK!" again she shouted, this time a little more desperately.

Placing a foot on a support, Lilith pulled herself up and peered into the storage locker. There she found a Parachute and several snowboards tossed about inside. Without hesitation, Lilith pulled herself into the locker and quickly strapped on a chute. Grabbing a Snowboard and clipping it on swiftly to her boots Lilith then pulled her pistol and fired several rounds into the cargo bay door's hydraulic system located under the copilot's seat. Super-heated hydraulic fluid burst everywhere instantly turning into a thick white smoke.

The cargo door burst open from the sudden release of pressure and swung on its hinges limp. Glass and debris rose up with an increased vengeance at the new supply of negative air pressure. Lilith pulled her goggles down over her eyes and rolled out of the locker letting the air current take her. Using the snowboard as a shield, she was able to negotiate the jagged metal rift without injury. She, regrettably, didn't have as much luck with the swinging cargo door.

At the mercy of the air current, Lilith plummeted board first down the cargo bay crouched at the knees just as the door began to swing closed. Almost as if she couldn't have timed it any worse the heaving door slammed into her body with sufficient enough force to knock her incoherent and take her breath away. Tumbling in the air, she clutched her chest guarding her lungs instinctively as she free fell barely aware of her situation. Acid burned in her lungs as the tension from the spasming muscle cramped, seizing her rib cage tight. Lilith knew that if she didn't get control of her breath that she could lose consciousness and die. Almost by instinct Lilith slowly slipped into a relaxed state of mind and tried to calm herself down long enough to take a breath. Falling limp for several seconds she was able to draw in a small breath, then another with just a little more air. It took her several moments, but finally, Lilith was able to breathe normally. Slightly calmer now that she could breathe and that she was able to escape the disintegrating cargo plane Lilith righted herself on the board and positioned herself into a comfortable stance.

Once situated, she glanced over her shoulder just in time to see the Cargo plane shatter apart just as she predicted. Fire and debris flowed away from the craft like a meteor entering the atmosphere.

Turning around, Lilith checked the area below and oriented herself to what she saw. Recognizing peek # UD3234459 on her Suunto GPS, she steered towards it and made herself comfortable. Lilith was 8,000 feet up and had some time on her hands. She survived. She made it. Now to calm down and enjoy the sites around her.

After roughly ten seconds or so into the run, Lilith noticed something odd, something that was going to complicate things. Again She closed her eyes in disgust.

Lilith had just passed what she recognized as the exhaust trails of two Hell Fire missiles and possibly a dozen or so tracer rounds that passed below her.

Both, she feared, from a Cobra helicopter just over her left shoulder.

"FUCK!" ...There's that word again.

Lilith spun to her left and drew her two handguns from her vest and her thigh holster. Targeting the Cobra, which was in a constant dive and way too close for comfort, she began to lay a swarm of, for lack of a better word, suppressive fire. There was no help from anyone now, and absolutely no cover was available.

The Cobra came within thirty feet of Lilith just before pulling away. The 45 caliber handguns would do little to the heavily armored vehicle, but then again, what could she do.

Slowing her decent, Lilith kept the Cobra in her sights and waited for the next assault with guns at the ready.

The Cobra spun on its axis and began to dive again. The 30mm cannon turned out more rounds as it closed in on its target. She grunted and groaned as she maneuvered around returning fire being careful not to hit her limbs as she flipped and spun dodging incoming fire.

As the Cobra came within range, Lilith returned fire but quickly ran out of ammo. She conducted a magazine exchange and emptied more rounds on her target. Again, to no effect.

The Cobra veered away again giving Lilith a chance to transition weapons. Letting the pistols go in the air Lilith pulled a double-barreled sawed-off shotgun from her waist pack at the base of her back and readied it. The shotgun was more of a tool than a weapon. Mostly used for breaching and barely ten inches long. She loaded one breaching round hoping it would at least cause enough damage to ward off the pilot.

As the Cobra came in, closer than before, Lilith was able to shower the left side of the craft with one good blast. Rounds burst and sparked finally piercing the heavy armor but caused no real damage. Promptly conducting a reload Lilith began maneuvering out of the way of the Cobra's auto cannons again.

Lilith and the Cobra faced off for a moment as if they were in an old western cowboy movie. Lilith, upright on her board, becoming very frustrated. Suddenly, the two advanced on each other with guns blazing. Lilith was clearly at a disadvantage.

When the Cobra came into range, Lilith concentrated on penetrating the canopy and taking out the pilot. She pulled the trigger smoothly and with little effort and the weapon surged in her grip. The rounds impacted against the Cobra's canopy cracking it. Elated that she had penetrated the defenses of the most elite combat aircraft in the world, she was doubly downhearted at the fact that she was now out of ammo.

"FUCK!" ...And again, that word.

Lilith grunting in frustration searched her plate carrier for ammo she knew she didn't have.

Completely hysterical at this point she threw the Shotgun in the direction of the Cobra as it veered away. To her surprise, the shotgun had traveled some distance before the wind caught it. Thinking quickly, she reached for one of two grenades. The timing would have to be perfect she thought while snickering at her devious plan.

A shit eating grin appeared on Lilith's face as the Cobra returned for round four of their fight for the sky. A barrage of cannon fire burst forth from the nose of the craft as it closed in for the kill. Lilith pulled the safety pin on the grenade and poised herself to fall as fast as she could.

Once the moment felt right, she let the trigger spoon go and counted to four on a five-second fuse. With all her might she threw the grenade straight for the pilot's face. As if in slow motion the grenade thumped against the canopy in front of the pilot's face and for a fraction of a seconded he realized his demise.

The grenade exploded as he looked on. The canopy imploded in a burst of black smoke and shrapnel. Flying debris, glass, and metal scythed through both the pilot and co-pilot from their seats. Blood, meat, metal and glass shot in all directions. Lilith sat back and admired her work as the Cobra began an uncontrolled spin towards the ground in a blazing flurry. Her satisfaction, however, was short-lived. Lilith abruptly realized she had no idea how close to the ground she was. Again, she raised an eyebrow in distress.

With her back to the ground, Lilith glanced over her shoulder and could see birds panicking out of the trees below. With a jerk, Lilith spun around and pulled her chute cord with a jolt.

The trees caught her chute and swung Lilith violently in a low arch just off the ground. Hitting Two quick releases by her hips Lilith eject from her harness at the last possible moment. The chute pulled taunt, and Lilith shot out of her harness. Flailing her arms back she launched from her harness and down a snowy slope at a quick sixty miles per hour pace.

She hit the slope of the mountain and desperately tried to stay upright. Cautiously Lilith veered away from the foliage on both sides of her and began negotiating several berms and hopping over logs and boulders. Lilith moved into an open area she noticed was part of a recreational slope. She felt safer now and was starting to have fun.

Several hundred yards down the slope, however, Lilith saw four men. All of which were armed to the teeth and fast roping out of a heavily armed BlackHawk. Not taking any chances as to who they were or how they got there she leaned into the board and gained speed. Voicing commands to her com system to search open frequencies Lilith kept a low profile as not to attract attention. She had one grenade and was not in the mood to play around anymore. As she came closer, the comm system beeped, and she heard a voice. The Voice was from somebody nearby and assumed it was the soldiers just down the hill.

Suddenly one soldier point at her and yelled into the mic at the same time to "Get Her!" All the other men, ten she thought, raise their weapons and began firing.

"Gatch Ya!" Lilith voiced aloud and pulled out her last grenade.

At incredible speed, she steered towards the group of men and kept a low profile as rounds impacted around her. She targeted the man that pointed her out thinking he just deserved it.

Approaching quick, Lilith held the grenade in her right hand and jerked the pin with her left. She then concentrated on placing herself on the left side of the guy that pointed her out. He seemed to have way too much motivation to kill her. And thus, he should go first. The hard way.

From only a few yards away Lilith threw the grenade as hard as she could into the chest of the soldier. The impact knocked him off his feet, and semi flipped in the air before he exploded. She estimated to herself that the impact speed would probably be around 180 mph or so. The impact alone should have killed him.

The other men were mowed down by the blast but injured only slightly. Shaking it off, they looked around trying to figure out what just happened. To them, their buddy just hopped up into the air and exploded. At the same time, a low-flying jet named Lilith flew over their heads at incredible speed.

Regardless, they began calling in an alert while trying to pick themselves up off the ground.

Lilith, however, was not slowing down much and began to worry. The semi-advanced ski slope she was on wouldn't stay straight for very long. Her speed compromised her ability to maneuver, turning to any degree, was risky. Falling and breaking a leg would not be a good thing at this point and she knew it.

Leaning back on the board slowed her down to a small degree but made her unstable and forced her to straighten. Once she straightened up, her speed increased.

As she contemplated her situation carefully, snow blasted her in the face by an unknown force. A jolt of electricity shot through her body from the surprise. She looked around at the cause and was not blissful about what she found.

A Bell CH 136 Kiowa Helicopter with two manned mini guns mounted outside her bay doors was moving into position fast behind Lilith, who suddenly realized now she wasn't going fast enough now.

Lilith looked around desperately for something to help her. Blasts of snow and dirt exploded around again as she risked to maneuver.

Out of the corner of her eye, she saw a sign that read *Warning! Do not cross!* The helicopter passed dangerously close overhead and blasted by like a hungry bird of prey. Lilith then launched herself off another berm jumping a chain link fence. Her attention, however, kept going back to the sign.

People don't put signs up unless they're trying to tell you something, Lilith thought to herself. She feared she had just made a huge mistake

Her subconscious kept nagging her about the importance of the sign as she maneuvered around trees and over boulders. Then, filled with dread like someone shot her dog, she realized her next situation.

Lilith saw the top of a suspension bridge just up a berm and steered towards it. Why shy away from the inevitable. In-between her and the bridge Lilith could now see Canyon about two hundred away and at least three hundred feet down ran a raging river.

"Fuck!" ...this is a useful word for her.

Ms. Robinson was a mild-minded and slightly naive 44-year-old 3rd-grade teacher from Utah. She had never been out of the state before, until now and was enjoying her well-earned vacation.

This vacation was also her first real adventure. Ever! When her plane left the airport, she made a promised to herself that she would do as many crazy things as she could before going home to her unadventurous life. Bungee jumping was one of them... or so she thought.

She opened her eyes again and looked directly at her Bungee instructor, Aanisah. It took Aanisah almost 15 minutes just to get her to hop over the railing of the bridge, and he couldn't get her to budge an inch more after that. Determined to get her to jump, Aanisah coaxed her a little more with a calm voice. The other tourist had already jumped, and Aanisah remembered that the last one off was always the hardest. But he will not be able to charge her a fee unless she jumps. Aanisah was planning to party this weekend with Maria, his new girlfriend. Who, by the way, has expensive tastes.

Ms. Robinson was very nervous and thought that there were other crazy things she could do as she listened to Aanisah. Her hands were wet and sore from holding onto the railing, and a little voice in her head decided that this was something she did not want to do anymore.

"It's that easy...Yes?" He said in his deep Igbo accent.

"No...I'm positive. This is something I don't think I really need to do." Her shaky voice whined.

Aanisah knew that it was all over and rolled his eyes. Pushing her any further would only adversely affect her vacation, and she would then tell all her friends not to come here and so on. The other tourist, however, began to urge her on which Aanisah did nothing about of course. Most were college students on vacation for the summer, and some were older than even Ms. Robinson.

Just then Aanisah saw something catch his attention across his peripheral vision. He did a double take and squinted trying to see what it was that caught his attention.

Scanning the ridge line, he could see trees jerk and small snowy dust clouds appear now and then. The burp of the Miniguns then began echoing in the canyon as everyone turned in the direction of the noise.

With a shocking surprise, Lilith comes blasting off the ridge at incredible speed. She tried to make the middle of the bridge road but came up short by about ten meters. The best she could do was the side of the bridge and to be honest; it wasn't a magnificent plan.

Lilith slammed against the bridge at an angle grinding the outermost railing with her board trying desperately to keep her balance. If she fell right, she had a 200-foot drop to icy cold rapids. To her left, steel beams, girders, and thick cable would easily dismember her at that speed. Neither of which would provide a soft landing. Her board produced hideous screeching sounds as she ducked beams and hopped over railing mounts. A sound so hideous everyone couldn't help but cover their ears.

Ms. Robinson saw the shock in Aanisah's eyes and quickly turned her attention to where he was looking. There she saw Lilith came at her like Spiderman on crack. Mr. Robinson gasped in shock but was unable to move. Fear blazed through her body like an electric shock. She drew in a deep breath to let out a scream, but it was too late. Ms. Robinson was a frail woman, and Lilith's densely packed athletic body would defiantly kill her on impact. However, going over the bridge would certainly kill Lilith. So Lilith went with the Win-win.

At breakneck speed and reacting off instinct Lilith mustered all her strength and pushed off the rail spinning 360 degrees around as not to slam into Ms. Robinson directly. Lilith then wrapped her arms and legs around Ms. Robinson's waist and shoulders as the momentum than ripping them both off the railing with such violence it blew Aanisah's hat off his head. Ms. Robinson started screaming bloody murder at this point. Her voice wailed at first and then trailing off as the two began to plummet into the gorge. Everyone else slowly walked to the railing and peered over in utter shock. Nobody was quite sure what just happened. Not even Aanisah.

As the group stood there in astonishment one of the faddishly dressed college student, apparently a football jock, shouted out abruptly.

"THAT WAS FUCKING SICK!"

No sooner than he finished explosive tipped mini-gun rounds began to impact the steel beams and girders around them. Sparks, fire, smoke, and noise, shattered the surreal ambiance as tourist panicked and sprinted in all directions utterly confused about what to do. Hot metal and fire relentlessly swarmed the area like an onslaught of rabid Hornets.

Lilith, of course, added way too much weight for the Bungee cord, and both Ms. Robinson and she hit the icy river with a shocking jolt. Once in the water, Lilith let poor Ms. Robinson go launching her out of the water like an intercontinental ballistic missile. Mr. Robinson recoiled from the water with such velocity she was able to re-grasped the railing she was just on and clenched it tight like a vise. Choking on the water but otherwise unhurt she swore that she would never leave Utah again.

Lilith kicked off the board and quickly swam to the surface for air. Breaching the water, she surveyed her situation. The helicopter was hovering 40 feet overhead. The crew chief was directing two men on jet-skies to her approximate position. No guns and out of grenades Lilith began to worry. Again...

The two men spotted her and were moving in fast. Lilith went under before the miniguns could open fire. She needed gear and the only two people with gear were en route. All Lilith had to do was hold her breath long enough. She calmed her thoughts and tried to relax as best she could. Her body was already starving for oxygen as is. She just needed a little more time.

The two jet skiers were a little confused. From what they could gather from the radio reports, someone bombed their quick reaction team shortly after their Air Weapons Team crashed while pursuing and destroying a freight Aircraft. And in all honesty, they did not know what to think about what just happened at the bridge. Following their orders, they cautiously moved in on the suspected area looking around nervously.

Laying in wait six feet under the water, Lilith held tightly to a jagged rock to keep from drifting downstream. As the Jet-skiers moved in just above her, she aguishly resisted the urge to inhale. One of the Jetskiers, taken by the current, floated over Lilith unwittingly. Taking advantage of the situation, Lilith quickly pulled her boot knife out and charged the surface.

Launching from the water on the far side of the Jet skier she grabbed the man by his shoulders and dragged him into the water simultaneously cutting his throat open. Lilith then quickly took the tactical vest and gun belt off the now dead. As she was readying herself, she looked up and noticed the other jet skier had jetted off in a panic. The crew in the helicopter just watched in astonishment unsure as to what to do.

Through the murky water, Lilith noticed she had acquired an M4 Carbine with an M203 40-mm grenade launcher attached to its lower frame. Not bad for free. In her newly acquired gun belt, she felt what she thought was a Sig Saur pistol probably a 9mm. With that in hand, she felt a little better and began to swim up to the surface towards the abandoned Jet Ski.

Making her way under the now unmanned Jet Ski, Lilith opened the M-203's tube and checked to ensure there was a round loaded. She surfaced the water and took a deep breath through her nose trying not to make too much commotion. With the tube still open to allow water to drain out she again leaped from the water and onto the jet ski laying the weapon over the seat. Lilith Angled the weapon down and quickly drained the M-203s tube of water, jacked it into firing position, and took aim on the helicopter.

As she did, two huge streams of water rose like giant rooster tails on both sides of her from helicopter's miniguns. Lilith pulled the trigger on the M203 shot the round with a single thump. She could see the projectile fly through the air and impact the helicopters right minigunner. The force of the explosion blasted through the aircraft pushing the other minigunner out the other side. Desperately clinging to his weapon, the Gunner inadvertently began to fire as he swung out of his seat and around his gun mount. This calamity sent hundreds of rounds into the canopy and engine of the helicopter killing the pilot and destroying the engines. The

Helicopter lurched backward as glass and metal fragments shot everywhere. The aircraft engines screamed as if someone placed them at full throttle. Seconds later it burst into flames as it slammed into the cliff wall creating a gigantic fireball.

"Whow!" Lilith shouted in astonishment covering her face from the heat of the blast. She didn't expect that to happen.

Lilith quickly reloaded and mounted her newly acquired ride. She then turned to and stared at her new opponent. Through dark shaded goggles and weapon in hand; Lilith just sat there with that 'Lookie what I just did' smirk on her face.

The second Jet skier just stared back unsure of what to do. He wasn't getting paid enough he thought. He was positive his skill set was nowhere near the level of Lilith's and today was not a good day to die for sure. So he decided to leave and move as quickly as he could. Gunning the throttle, he heading downstream like a shot.

Lilith, giving chase, knew she needed information on what was going on and decided he was a good start. She spun the Jet Ski around and opened fire at the mortified man with a volley of rounds. Lilith chased after him finally feeling back in control and on the offensive.

Both Lilith and the other jet skier shot down the winding river, which at the time was rather calm and wide. Cliffs of solid rock surrounded them on both sides providing no escape but downstream and super fast. Lilith targeted the other jet skier as best she could, firing at him when possible. The farther they went down the river, though, the faster the current increased. Rocks and white water began to form making shooting accurately difficult. The opposing jet skier had a good fifty-meter lead on her and since they both had the same type of Jet Ski Lilith couldn't catch up as quickly as she would like. This mission was highly unusual even for her. She needed answers, and so did her command.

Lilith had to end and end it soon.

The river was way too rough to make a decent shot and Lilith didn't want to waste ammunition, so she slung her weapon and focused on closing the distance. She would wait for a long straightaway in the river to stop and sight properly before making her next shot. About a hundred meters down the river the rapids became calm and the width of the river opened up.

This is it! She thought as she let off the throttle and quickly leveled her weapon. Taking careful aim, she let her breath out slow and then held it. With the iron-sights on her target, she began to squeeze the trigger. Suddenly, that warm and fuzzy feeling left again, and Lilith lowered her weapon slightly dropping her gaze and listened.

Silence, at first. Then abruptly Lilith heard a large motorboat at full throttle and looked over her shoulder. There she saw a Red Firehawk speed boat coming in fast. Mounted on her deck was a manned twin .50 caliber machine gun rig trained in her general direction.

"Are you fucking kidding me?!"

Lilith reached for another 40mm grenade and jacked the M-203's tube forward. As she did, the distinctive and repetitious thumping of the big guns rang in her ears. Rooster tails reared from the water and up the cliff wall. Cursing, Lilith dropping the grenade and slammed the throttle forward launching the jet ski and her downstream. Lilith's only hope for survival was dropping down low and running like hell. Frustrated and angry she half laughed at the situation trying to release some stress. But to no avail... she was pissed.

The Firehawk is an incredibly fast boat, and the .50 calibers had a range of at least a thousand meters. Its range and speed made the craft a highly formidable foe. Grabbing the rifle's sling, Lilith tightened it up so that the weapon was secure under her arm and facing forward.

More rounds came in shredding the surface of the river. The large caliber rounds impacted the water with such ferocity Lilith could feel the shock wave through the hull of the jet ski. Anticipating impact, she pulled up on the ski, then drove the entire craft and herself nose first into the water. The machine gun rounds were going too fast, and at such a slight angle to the water, they skipped off the surface and into the cliff wall. Once under water, Lilith forced the nose of the craft up by throttling the motor thrusting the craft up to the water's surface like a torpedo. As she did, Lilith grabbed the rifle's grip with one hand and turned the ski's steering to the right with the other. The tight turn gave her a slight spin as she reached the surface.

Bounding out of the water Lilith blasted rounds in the direction of the speedboat. One shot hit the windshield of the boat shattering it. The boat driver shocked from the incoming rounds jerked the boat left trying to avoid further impacts. Throttling the ski, Lilith headed back downstream again.

The other skier, feeling more confident about his situation, turned his craft upstream and raced towards Lilith. Seeing this Lilith conducted a magazine exchange on the rifle with her left hand and drew her pistol with her right. Laying down suppressive fire with the pistol Lilith finished her magazine exchange and opened up on the jet skier with the rifle. Rounds slammed into the chest and side of the other skier. With puffs of red mist, he fell into the water, dead.

"Fuck with me guy!"

Lilith then sped off as fast as she could. The speedboat driver finally got the boat's nose around and throttled up as the Gunner took aim and opened fire once more. The river was going much faster and more curvaceous. Maneuvering became increasingly difficult. Lilith kept the Jet Ski to the inside wall as a defensive measure. The cliff wall gave her much-needed cover from her adversary.

"Mother fu…" she whispered to herself.

However, this tactic would not last long, and Lilith was feeling the effects of such a long struggle. She was fatigued and extremely frustrated. Every victory smashed by a grave let down. Her body ached, her mind exhausted and her will was at the breaking point. And as she had fear Lilith ran out of curves rather abruptly and came up to a ten-foot waterfall that opened up to a small reservoir. Her heart sank yet again. She now knew it was time to take significant risks. She was down on the mat with ten seconds to go and if she continued the way she was she would eventually lose it all. Time lay it all out!

"Fuck it!"

Wrenching on the hard throttle, Lilith attempted to gain as much speed as possible could. Hitting the crest of the waterfall she launched the Jet Ski into the air like a rocket. Angling the nose of the vehicle down Lilith impacted the water's surface nose first. Spinning the Jet Ski around, she nailed the throttle again. Once she breached the water, she heading back upstream. Just in time too. The Firehawk exploded off the ridge of the waterfall blasting water in all directions. Lilith crouched low and slipped under the Firehawk before it could crush her. The massive boat propellers nearly shredding her as she escaped from underneath the fast moving boat.

Lilith jerked the ski around and raced up behind her pursuer's unloading her rifle on the boat with bullets. The driver turned abruptly attempt to evade the assault. Several rounds skimmed his thigh. The Gunner, however, tried to turn his large weapon around only to discover its mount locked up at ninety degrees. In a panic, he hit the deck for cover. The driver, in pain but otherwise unharmed, punched the throttle and ran like hell downstream.

Sensing his impending doom, the driver called in for backup by directing two Bell CH-136 Kiowa helicopters in their direction both armed to the teeth. Estimating their time of arrival at three minutes, the boat driver concentrated on the rocks and Lilith, who was giving chase. He just had to stay alive long enough for the chopper to get there.

The Gunner feeling too exposed on the deck unlatched himself and made his way to the rear of the boat as best he could. Stumbling, he retrieved an old Russian PKM machine-gun in a cargo hold under the back seat. Trying desperately to hold the heavy weapon and still keep his balance the Gunner clumsily returned fire. Lilith made evasive maneuvers avoiding the incoming round and white water. Lilith then slowed down and increased the distance between her and the boat. Distance and the turbulent water made the PKM's fire almost ineffective. Lilith then returned cover fire keeping the pressure on the pursuing attackers to prevent them from turning on. Now that she's upstream from her adversary and the machine gun unable to turn on her, she felt in control again. Things were looking good. But, of course, this didn't last too long.

The helicopters arrived and announced their presence with a massive onslaught of minigun round impacting the water around her. The canyon walls were too narrow to accommodate the helicopters, so the Gunners peppered the area with gunfire in hopes of making a lucky hit. Lilith began evading the bullets as best she could keeping close to the canyon walls for as much cover as possible. She braced for impact as she slammed into the canyon wall while hundreds of rounds blasted the rock above her. Solid rock and rubble began to tumble on top of her as maneuvered the JetSki out of the way. Her brain started buzzing for a way out as she drove the Jet Ski back underwater for badly needed cover. Rooster tails of water rose up from three different directions where she disappeared. When she resurfaced, she let go of the jet ski's steering controls and covered her face with her hands. She was at her breaking point. She was about to give up. Breathing heavy she felt like she should just let it happen. She was almost out of fuel and ammo. Her body beaten and exhausted and her mind about to crack. She thought maybe it was better. She dropped her hands off her face and rested them in her lap. She couldn't muster the energy to go on. But when she looked up she knew her fate was sealed. She was slowly drifting out of the river mouth and into the open Pacific Ocean.

She had unknowingly traveled twenty-five miles downstream during her little getaway and reached the open ocean. With her cover gone and the fact that her vehicle was too slow to outrun the Firehawk and the helicopters, her situation became dreary.

She remembered a time when she was in Israel learning grappling from an amazing man named Dani. Dani redefined fighting into an art form. This guy could kill anyone within 10 meters with only a few steps or moves. Dani was quick, strong and very deadly. One of the things he taught her was that there was no good time to fight. Nobody will ever be ready for battle or even in the mood. When you need to fight the most is when you don't have anything left to give. To survive, you had to kill your opponent within one or two moves. You did this because that's all you had left in the tank. His warm-ups lasted an hour to an hour and a half before any training began. She trained exhausted and to the point of passing out. Dani however, expects you to fight till everyone was dead. One, two sometimes four opponents would be attacking. And you would keep doing the drill till you got it right. No water breaks, no latrine breaks, and no time to come up with a plan. Life doesn't give you a break. Only death will.

She stood up on her craft. Trying to look defeated Lilith put her arms straight out to her side and dropped the rifle into the ocean. Then, reaching slowly she grabbed her side arm and dropped it into the sea as well. Drifting, she waited.

As the helicopters made their way around, the boat driver radioed for them to back off and kept them from firing on her. He then advised the helicopters that he was going to bring the target in for "interrogations." Bringing Lilith in, the boat driver thought, would bring him a good bounty maybe. Lilith also might have some useful information his superiors could use to their advantage. Maybe they could have a little fun with her before they killed her as well he thought.

As he chuckled under his breath, the boat driver throttled forward slightly. The M2 Gunner now trained on Lilith and was ready for anything. Lilith could hear the rumble of their motor pulling up alongside her slowly and tried to look as defeated as possible. The boat driver pulled a gun from his holster and pointed it at her.

"Climb aboard, SLOWLY!" He ordered with a Spanish accent.

Lilith did what she was told.

"Lay down on the floor and place your hands on top of your head!" The boat driver ordered again. The M2 Gunner then grabbed his sidearm and drew down on Lilith. As Lilith boarded the boat, she made sure she was facing the Gunner. She then dropped to her knees and slowly laid face down on the deck placing her hands on her head. The boat driver then looked at the Gunner to ensure he was covering him. The Gunner nodded his assurance as the boat driver pulled a couple of wire harness straps from a tool box. He then placed his weapon in his holster and fashioned a pair of makeshift handcuffs from the straps. Once satisfied with his clever device the boat driver straddled Lilith's lower back and reached for her right wrist. Mistake number one, Lilith thought. And let the slaughter begin.

Lilith let the boat driver bring her wrist to the small of her back with no resistance. Once there, Lilith flipped her wrist around while grabbing the boat driver's hand and flipped over on her back with a jerk thus placing a wrist lock on him. At the same time, Lilith snatched the sidearm from the driver's holster with her free hand. While kicking the driver forward, she spun to her knees with a flash. The Gunner, shocked from the sudden activity, fired off a round and accidental shot the driver in the head killing him instantly.

Lilith then pushed the now dead boat driver forward into the boat's dash and emptied a full magazine into the body and chest of the Gunner. She then sprinted across the vessel to the twin M2's, pushed the Gunner out of the way, and trained the guns on the closest helicopter to her.

The Helicopters were already on the move with minigunners firing. Lilith snatched the M2's up and returned fire. Plumes of water and boat fragments exploded around her, but Lilith focused her thoughts on her two closing targets.

Chung Chung Chung Chung. Lilith churned the big twin guns like a mindless machine.

Round after round she pounded the body of the closest helicopter. Pieces of boat and wood began to splinter and impelled into her body. The nearest helicopter began to break apart, so Lilith turned her attention to her next threat. The second helicopter shot overhead, and Lilith pelted its underbelly with the last of her rounds. Within seconds, it burst into flames. The first helicopter began to auto-rotate into the water just to Lilith's right about fifty meters away with the right minigunner still firing. Lilith then swung the rig around and concentrated fire on him ripping him apart. Looking over her shoulder, Lilith saw the other helicopter crash into the water and explode. Good timing too, she thought. The Firehawk was now completely under the water and sinking fast. Conducting a quick inventory, she had about five rounds left.

She began to tread water and desperately tried to find the Jet Ski that she hoped was nearby. It too had been damaged during the firefight, but it still ran... barely. Lilith swam over to the crippled crafted as it struggled to idle. She then mounted its shredded seat and at a slow throttle headed for the deep ocean. From a small ankle pouch, Lilith pulled out a small waterproof satellite phone and called in SitCom.

"Control this is Slaughter. Beginning coding now." She ordered.

"Coding initiated." The Operator announced. Lilith pulled the phone away from her ear and waited for the coding to initiate. Suddenly Lilith could hear Joey's voice.

"God damn! What's your situation?"

"Piece of cake man. I'm all good!" she was lying of course as she scanned the horizon for new threats Then suddenly she could hear everyone in SitCom let out a thunderous victory shout!

"fuckin ah! I know you're hurting, but everyone here is a complete wreck!" he gasped. Lilith heard a voice in the background she assumed was the CIA rep stated that he needed a drink.

"I could use one too! Where's my out?" Lilith asked.

"Oh yeah... LISTEN UP!" Joe began shouting at the SitCom crew. "Let me connect you..." Joey then placed Lilith on hold and transferred the call to the waiting sub. He was never a guy you could just sit and talk to.

"This is Captain Richards. Go ahead!" The new voice answered.

"This is Slaughter. I Authenticate Bravo 1276." Lilith returned.

"I Authenticate X-ray 3475. Where are you?" Lilith then began to search for her GPS device and notice she had lost it along with most of her gear and her Suunto watch.

"I'm not sure. Go to 'periscope up' and look for me. I shouldn't be far."

"Stand By!" The Captain answered.   Lilith then stood up on her Jet Ski and began looking to her right and into deeper ocean. As she scanned for the Subs scope for several minutes, she heard a humming noise to her left. She turned her head and yelped at what she saw. The scope was not more than a couple of inches from her jet ski, and it scared the daylight out of her.

"HOLD ON! HOLD ON!" She shouted into the phone. But the submarine kept rising. Lilith then throttled the Jet Ski quickly and stalled it.

"Fuck it." She protested, completely drained from her escape. Just then the Observation Deck began to rise out of the water and right under her. The wall of the deck capsizes the ski and Lilith went straight into the deck's bay. She floated there for several seconds while the observation deck drained out. After a moment or two, Lilith felt her body relax and slowly went to her knees. She cupped some water in her hands and poured it over her head.

"Son of a... "

CHAPTER 3
"Why I am."

Africa, six years earlier…

"This rain sucks! Over." Dave stated breaking the half hour of radio silence.

"At least it's not cold. Remember Ukraine? Over" Joe replied

"Ah, but the food was good! And by food I mean Ivanka. Over" Dave laughed. "I don't think I have ever been that tired in my life."

"Mother fucker…. Alright everyone call in status."

Joe rolled to one side and checked the map he was laying on. As each position verbally checked in, Joe made a mental note of their status until he was satisfied everyone was good. Joe then pulled the hood of his gilly suit off and reached in a small hole in the ground. There he found one of two radios. Changing the channel on one of the radios, Joe called in his report.

"Roman Base this Predator, Over."

"Go ahead Predator." a voice returned.

"Still no target. Are you sure we're at the right place."

"That's a roger. We were told the convoy is on the move and should be there by now. Maybe the target got held up. Break." Joe pulled up a pair of binos and scanned a small house in the distance.

"Get comfy; you may be there for a while." Everyone on the net heard that and sighed shaking their heads. It happens sometimes; Intel gets mixed up, and you end up on station for hours just to find out you've been surveying a chicken ranch and not a terrorist training camp. Following orders, Joe put the binos down and got comfy.

Just then the radio crackled to life, and everyone's hearts jumped.

"Predator this is Creeper we've got movement. Three trucks inbound, escorting a merc. Over." Dave stated

"Roger, all units prep for action. Break." Joe ordered.

"Roman Base did you copy?" Joe continued.

"Roger, stand by for green on target confirmations."

Hours before Joe and Dave bugged the small house. Intel stated that a high-value terrorist target was going the small barn house to have a meeting with a major drug lord to arrange a trade agreement. Tactics like this are a common trend in terrorist activity, sell drugs to Americans to fund a war against Americans. Joe huffed at the idea as he pulled his binos out again.

The three trucks pulled up to the house and took up positions on the perimeter while the Mercedes parked right in front. Joe trained on the Mercedes trying to get a good look at the passengers when suddenly he heard a shriek.

He looked to his left and saw a group of armed men pulling a young girl with blazing red hair not much older than 18 out of the back of a truck. The young girl had blood on her face, down her blouse and dress and was not happy to be there.

"No fucking way! Joe… What the fuck?" Joe knew it was Dave, and he was aware that the girl was going to be entertainment for the VIP.

"All units hold!" Roman base added. They also could see via drones circling above and knew what was about to happen.

The girl, being dragged, screamed and kicked all the way house with the armed men taunting her in tow. One man kept slapping her in the ass and laughed viscously. They then stood her up next to the Mercedes. Two men to either side and one behind holding her head up. She shuddered and wept. The two men scolded and slapped her for crying out loud. Joe could tell she was trying to calm down, but fear and emotion had the best of her.

"Joe…!"

"Hold your position…" Joe stated. However, he didn't sound very convincing.

The doors of the Mercedes opened up, and four men got out. Two dressed in suits and one in a keffiyeh and solid OD green military uniforms. The Other was the driver dressed in casual wear. All four stepped up to the girl with wide grins. The man in the smock pulled out a knife and moved in close to the girl.

He said something and place the knife to her throat and slowly dragged the tip down her chest to her crotch.

"JOE.......!" The stress in Dave's voice resonated in Joe's ear like a bolt of electricity. His hands shook, his heart pounded, everyone's heart pounded. You could almost see the steam from their rage bellowing from their positions. All twelve men white knuckled their weapons waiting for the go. Their mission was to capture these guys not to kill them, but at that point, they started to hate their jobs.

The man in the smock said something, and the girl answered. However, it seems it wasn't the answer he was looking for and immediately became irate and began to yell.

"Just for that bitch... I'll make sure everyone gets a turn!" He then reached down and pulled up her dress and furiously yanked her panties off and threw them in her face. All the men let out a yell of approval and dragged her into the house as she bellowed out a muffled scream. An older man then began shouting angrily, ordering several men back to their positions. Once satisfied security was established he moved inside and joined in the festivities.

Dave started swearing brutally under his breath while tapping the trigger guard of a viciously modified HK rifle.

Joe laid there with his head down fuming with rage. His hands; clutching the earth, he could hear the leather creak as his grip tightened. Then he heard the door slam shut; time stopped, and everything went silent, deafeningly silent.

After a moment, Joe heard something. A sound... no! A voice from deep within his mind. It was quiet at first but got louder and louder. The sound became so loud that it made his head ache, and his body tremble. He couldn't 'Not' listen to it anymore.

"KILL!!"

Joe could hear the Crack that came afterward! It was excruciatingly loud. He wasn't sure if it was in his head or not. It didn't matter. The choice was made.

"Creeper! Sweep East to West... All units Green! Green! Green!" Joe shouted into the radio as he bolted from the wood line in a dead sprint.

Dave, letting out a loud battle cry, let fly twelve rounds of explosive tip 7.62 mm rounds from his rifle in less than 6 seconds as Joe raced across an open field with ten other team members in tow. Joe couldn't hear the shots, but he could see the twelve small pink puffs pop out of the heads of the twelve guards just like he asked... from East to West.

Once the command was complete, Dave dropped his weapon and launched from his position pulling his Sig 1911 from his chest rig and sprinted to the house. Several men came running out in a panic. Dave and Joe, quick on the triggers, fired five rounds each without hesitation dropping them only feet from their exit.

Closing in on the house fast, Dave noticed something that would stick with him for the rest of his life. That moment, as if in slow motion, still burns in his mind. He didn't know what he saw at first, but his subconscious did. As he got closer to the house still at a full sprint, he noticed blood on the windows. Not just a little blood, a grotesquely large amount of dark arterial blood. Shaking the sight off, Dave came up to the south side of the house and sprinted around the corner linking up with Joe. Joe slammed into the front door with such force the door splintered into thousands of pieces. Moving against the right wall, Dave pulled in behind while the rest of the team began staggering left and right once in the door. The dynamic entry action halted quickly once the team members got inside and got a good look around.

In a line, shoulder to shoulder stood the entire team. Just standing there in awe, weapons to their sides, breathing heavy… just staring.

The inner room was rather large with an old wood floor and furnished with only a couple small tables and some chairs. The ceiling was vaulted crisscrossed with large wooden beams accented by two old ceiling fans that turned slowly making a rhythmic squeaking noise.

The girl with the red hair stood in the middle of the room with her back to the door. She wasn't startled when the team entered. She knew who they were before they entered and did not fear them.

Her dress was torn exposing her leg. In her right hand, she held a bayonet style knife. But that wasn't the surprising part. The girl was covered head to toe in blood. Not a little… a lot! Blood covered the entire floor. Bodies and body parts laid randomly about the room as if a grenade blasted them apart. There was so much blood several of the team members had to hold onto other team members to keep from slipping and regain their stance. Blood splattered the walls and dripped off the ceiling beams. At least fifteen men died inside the house and only the girl, relatively unharmed, survived.

"FUCK ME!" a team member blurted out loudly breaking the silence.

The girl turned around slowly and looked at the team expressionless. Everyone took a step back and slightly raised their weapons unsure as to what was about to happen. After about a second or two Dave stepped forward and held out his hand.

"Um, my name is Dave... Uh.. Are you hurt?"

"Lilith..." The girl said with a shaky voice.

The girl gazed at Dave as if she could see through him and at that moment began to falter. Dave closed the distance seeing what was about to happen. Her eyes rolled up, and she passed out. Dave, just barely able to get to her in time, caught her.

CHAPTER 4
"Strange Conflict"

Present day...

The five up-armored Suburbans shot down the highway in a tight formation and at least 20 mph over the speed limit. Joe is driving the lead vehicle with Dave navigating in the passenger seat. The convoy resembled a runaway freight train barreling down the highway. Not that anyone would have noticed in the middle of the forest at midnight. Ten of the twelve team members were on board. The last Two were out of contact in Vegas somewhere. Val and Monty were always finding trouble. Most of the time a young hottie was in distress, and then all hell breaks loose. Although last time they did take down a Russian Crime Syndicate in Chicago but were banned from ever returning as well. That was the last time they were out. He suspects they were in jail or at least hoped so. They've done it before... Always mocking the dragon in its face. Well, he needed them worse than the local PD did and placed them on the Homeland Security's most wanted list for interviewing. He hoped to secure them as soon. The ten other team members were at least here, and in good spirits, Joe thought. Until...

"Uhhh!" Lilith grunted aloud waking from one of her frequent and disturbing nightmares.

"Damn... You OK?" Joe asked from the front seat.

Lilith looked around and after a moment nodded yes. Jack, a large, dark and an unusually hairless man, placed his hand on Lilith's thigh in assurance.

"We got you." He stated in a thick African accent.

"I know..." Lilith responded in appreciation sitting up in her seat.

Central Command called the entire team in for an emergency meeting just a few days after Lilith's little conflict in South America. She assumed it was because of the heavy presence in the area. Not many Special Operatives meet that kind of resistance even on a mission like hers. Attack helicopters and Speed Boats were not among the usual response. Everyone knew something was way wrong with that whole thing but couldn't pinpoint the reasoning.

"Dreams again...?" Jack asked

"Yeah... seem worse now for some reason."

"Worse? They seemed pretty bad before." Jack stated somewhat surprised.

Jack was the only one Lilith talked to about her dreams and her feelings. No shrinks, no drugs. She tried in the past, but the shrinks seemed contradicting, and the drugs only antagonized her or blurred her sense of the world. She liked to be sharp, and drugs clouded that.

"These are strange, though. Monsters...
creatures appearing from nowhere... or something like
that. A huge cave" She looked at Jack with a worried
face.

"Interesting. Nothing like the dreams you had
before. What do you think they mean?" Jack asked.

"Nothing good..." she confessed.

Jack searched for words. *Nothing good* usually
meant that nothing good was about to happen. He
patted her thigh in assurance and left it at that. As he
did Lilith turned her attention to the darkness outside.
She was in the back of luxurious up-armored Suburban
and couldn't see much but kept looking anyway. No
street lights for miles. The darkness swallowed the
forest just a few steps in. Unless it was three feet from
the truck, you couldn't see it. Then again she wasn't
looking either. Her mind was drifting miles away back
to her dreams.

She dreamed about amazing places and
fantastic landscapes that seemed to go on forever.
And the creatures she stumbled upon in these
landscapes looked so unimaginable twisted. She
sometimes felt she was going crazy. She couldn't
understand how her mind came up with these images.
Even the conversations with these outlandish being
seemed bizarre. Most she would battle, but a few felt
familiar as if she had a deep connection to them. They
were even polite and respectful as if she was royalty.
She thought she was about to go to sleep when
suddenly something caught her attention. She didn't

see it or hear it, but more of less felt something. That something felt horribly wrong.

Jack, sitting next to her, glanced over and noticed how uneasy she looked.

"Hey… You Ok?"

Lilith snapped out of her daze and looked at Jack. She was a little startled but tried not to look it. Jack was the team's interrogator, and she knew he picked up on it, lying would only insult his intelligence. His sense of empathy was creepy accurate.

She began to explain herself when she seemed to have noticed something outside Jacks window. A flash of something but she knew she saw it. It was broken and unnatural, soulless…

Jack noticed her sudden and intense interest and sat up straight in his seat trying to get out of the way from her gaze. He wanted to look but didn't think he wanted to see what was there. He knew that look meant trouble. Lilith leaned towards him and began to squint. The urge to look was almost overwhelming. However, the fear of what he would find was stronger. His eyes grew bigger as she leaned in closer.

"Joe…" He grunted in a soft voice. Joe, driving, didn't hear Jack's call and kept on his route. Then suddenly the headlights from behind them shined in the cabin of the vehicle just long enough for Jack to notice the pistol in Lilith's hand.

"JOE!" Jack grunted again louder followed by a backhand to Dave's head.

"...ut the fuck!" Dave cursed looking behind him. There he notices Lilith in her hyperintense gaze.

"Shit.... Head's up we're not alone!" Dave announced over his throat mic as Joe began to slow down.

Everyone in the convoy jumped and grabbed whatever weapon they could muster and loaded it. Confused at the order, everyone knew that something was up, or Dave wouldn't have said anything. Lilith must be up to her old magic again they thought.

Up ahead Joe noticed a glow on the horizon and whacked Dave on the arm. Dave looked at Joe and then down the road. Squinting, he saw it too.

"Fuck she's good!" He stated aloud.

Lilith leaned forward in-between Dave and Joe to see what they saw. What she found just up the road confused her.

"Is that a street light?" Dave asked.

Lilith grabbed Joe's shoulder.

"Stop here. Don't go any further. It's an ambush!"

Joe slammed on the breaks with no warning to the others. All four vehicles slammed into one and other with their breaks locked up. Smoke erupted from their wheel wells as the tire screeched the convoy to a halt.

"Backup! Online! Twenty meters! GO!" Joe yelled over the radio.

Lilith with one swift movement leaned back in her seat and kicked the sunroof out sending the heavy glass shield flying through the air.

Everyone, although quite aware of the fact that Lilith just threw out a 4-inch thick ballistic shielding humbly disguised as a sunroof from atop their armored vehicle with just her legs made no attempt as to try to reason or understand how that was possible. They were still chewing on the ambush thing. One thing at a time they thought.

Joe slammed the vehicle into reverse and waited for everyone to backup out of his way. He didn't have to wait long. Once the truck hit the twenty-meter line, they veered off left and right and eventually were aligned four wide on the road.

Lilith took up a tactical position out the sunroof while Dave and Jack popped out their windows and began laying suppressive fire in every direction, as did the others once online.

Joe slammed the vehicle into park and quickly exited the driver's door and motioned Jack to move up. Once in position, Jack continued to fire while Joe retrieved two smoke grenades from in the back of his seat and tossed them in front of the vehicles for camouflage. Masked under the smoke, everyone stopped firing and reloaded their weapons.

"Blackout! Snipers post! Crew serves at the flanks! Jack with me! Lilith get the fuck down here!" Joe shouted and no sooner than he finished his commands everyone posted. Lilith and Jack went to the back of their vehicle, and Joe handed them both a thermal device. All three then moved to the front of the convoy and began scanning for heat signatures.

The smoke grenades started to fizzle out, and Joe held up Two fingers from a balled fist. Two team members hurled out more smoke grenades to continued the convoys mask.

"I can see movement... but no heat... I can't tell what it is..." Jack whispered.

"They're there for sure... I know it!" Lilith whispered back.

"That light post is only a post with a light... Where are the fucking transformers or power source?" Jack noted.

"Snipers... Recon by Fire." Joe ordered. No sooner did he complete his sentence when two high-powered rifles fired a single shot each.

They waited.

"I fucking hit something..." Dave exclaimed.

"I did to..." Jason, with a thick English accent, confirmed his shot as well.

The smoke grenades began to fizzle out again, and Joe held up a fist with no finger. He wanted to draw the enemy out and let them see the convoy. They waited again for a minute or two.

Joe then pulled a night vision optic from his vest and attached it just in front of his ACOG Sight. A faint high pitched whine broke the silence that quickly faded as Joe raised his weapon and sighted down the road.

The street light blazed in his optics like a blowtorch burning metal. He could faintly see an object just down the road maybe twenty meters or so. It appeared to have a human form but lumbered up to the light unnaturally... eerily. Joe breathed in deep as it stepping into the light deliberately almost tauntingly.

There in the light drenched in a sickly green hue was a man...a soldier of sorts. His stature was large and ominous, with large armored shoulder and chest plate, a long black coat with a swastika that blazed the entire right side of its chest and down the right coat leg. Its head, hooded and faced down, rose slowly towards Joe as he squinted to get a better look at it. It slowly reached up removed its hood then grasped the front of a full faced helmet underneath the hood and removed it as well. As the man lowered the helm to his side, he looked straight at Joe. Joe lowered his weapon and looked past the sights into the darkness. The orange glow was far and the thing next to it almost unrecognizable as a person. He couldn't believe what he saw.

"What the fuck is that Joe? That's not right!" Jason stated nervously over the coms.

Joe then quickly readjusted his stance and grip and looked down the sights again.

The thing he saw had no hair to speak of, and its skin was a putrid pale waxy color. Its face appeared thick and bony. His eyes were black, dark and piercing, filled with rage and contempt. His mouth, lower jaw, and nose were obscured by what appeared to be an armored plated mask. He then raised his hand and began to motion for Joe to come forward, tauntingly.

Lilith suddenly dropped to her knees and placed her palm on the ground. Joe glanced over to see what the fuss was about and when he saw Lilith, he motion for someone to help her. Jack moved in as Joe looked down his sights again. As he did, the man... or thing... turned and walked away limping slightly. There, on its back, was a giant armor plate with a large swastika displayed on it.

"Armor... Left flank!" Lilith announced.

"Mount up!" Joe shouted, and everyone began cursing and jumped into the nearest vehicle. As they maneuvered back to the trucks, a cracking sound began to emerge from up on the ridgeline to their left, shortly followed by the roar of a powerful diesel motor. This roar quickly broke the calm of the forest and began hammering in the ears of the group like a thousand drum. Everyone on the left side of the vehicles started laying suppression, and the four trucks launched down the road.

"Suppress 10 and 2!" Joe ordered over the radio, and a blaze of fire shot out from the 10 o'clock to the 2 o'clock of the convoy as they gouged their way through what was once the original ambush point. Sporadic gunfire erupted all around, but the majority of the ambush was just cresting the ridge in an attempting to flank them. Just where Lilith said they would be.

"Armor 7 o'clock 200 meters!" Jack yelled out. Dave echoed the call to the others and ordered the rear vehicle to take action. Fergus, a large Irish meat and potatoes kind of guy, lumbered to the rear of the Suburban and attempted to retrieve one of two AT4 rocket's buried in the back. Everyone else turned their fire to the crest of the hill and engaged what enemy they could see.

Joe, a history buff, recognized the armored vehicle cresting the hill as an old Panzer Jaeger 1. This tank, however, was modified with a twin cannon turret, which the original Jaegers did not have. This one seemed larger as well. Originally the Panzer Jaeger 1 was used initially as an anti-infantry vehicle in the later days of the WWII. What the hell it was doing here, however, Joe had no idea. How did this thing get here may have been a better question? Joe suspected some white supremacies group must have acquired one and are attempting to start some jacked up Race War. But that soldier just wasn't right. It didn't move normal... natural...

The Panzer crested the ridge with a thud and began to train its turret in the direction of the convoy loudly clunking as it did. Black smoke, burning embers, and steam rose from every crack and crevice of its armor. Joe hit the accelerator, and the others followed reaching 100 mph plus quickly.

"Where are the fucking rockets?" Joe demanded.

"They're under my bloody bridges and things, Sir. My fault for not planning on using the rockets against the Nazi's while roaming the countryside and all." Fergus stated in an all too sarcastic voice.

Joe just winced and shook his head.
The convoy reached the light post at blinding speed. Joe tried to scan the area for the thing that coaxed him on, but there was no sign of it anywhere.

"SHIFT FIRE… REAR!" Joe shouted into the mic. The order was odd since normally the command only goes left or right, but everyone knew what he meant and smirking as they turned to the rear. He knew he would get shit for that one later.

The team did what they were told and began providing suppressive fire to the rear of the convoy taking care not to shoot the vehicles and men behind them. Although highly ineffective they continued, and Joe knew it would be. The two center vehicles moved to opposing sides of the road from each other as to add weaponry to the fight. The teams signaled that they were out of ammo and needed to reload. Signaling a confirmation, the two trucks changed sides and began their suppression with new Gunners.

"Hurry with the fucking rockets, Fergus." Joe exclaimed.

"Got one Sir!"

"You wanna shoot the tank now?"

Fergus was having a horrible time getting situated in the back of the truck with such a large weapon and his huge ass body. Cursing loudly, he dug for space throwing gear bags and hard cases to the middle seat.

The Jaeger breached the drainage ditch and landed on the road like an angry bull looking for a fight, its torrent already trained on the convoy.

Fergus pulled the shipping pins on the AT4 and quickly tethered himself to the rear seat latch. Then with a double-barreled shotgun blew out the upper rear hatch hinge.

The World War two Jaeger's could reload its main gun about one round every 35 seconds. But this was a cursed Jaeger from another place not like here and could turn out ten rounds at the same time per cannon. With a high engine rev, it began churning out its deadly barrage of artillery lobbing its load at the convoy.

Thump Thump Thump!

"INCOMING!" Jack shouted. All Gunners quickly moved into their vehicles and rolled up all their windows for cover. Fergus let out a bloody war cry and with a mighty kicked out the rear hatch window off the truck and into the road. He then very ungracefully then leaned out of the rear of the vehicle placing one foot on the bumper.

Rounds began impacting all around the convoy in a relentless assault. Although the Jaeger had a difficult time staying on target, its measure of shots fired would eventually destroy the convoy soon enough.

Fergus raised the weapon and flipped the sights up.

"Hold her steady Mac!"

"Trying! But it isn't easy here!"

Several rounds impacted right next to the second vehicle raising the truck up on two wheels almost flipping it. The driver regained control and slammed it down on two bare rims. Sparks exploded all about and severely slowed their escape.

"GIVE HIM SOME HELP!" Joe yelled. Just then vehicle three and four jammed their accelerators to the floor. With engines roaring at full torque as they slammed into the back of the disabled truck to keep it at speed. Smoke and sparked erupted from the right side creating a wake of burning sparks and embers twelve feet high.

"This isn't going to last long Joe!" Dave yelled into the mic.

"Just a little farther out of the Kill Zone!" Joe replied.

Fergus was finally able to get the lumbering weapon out of the vehicle to safely fire it off. However, he was barely able to hold onto it with all the turbulence from the wind and fodder from the tank rounds. With all his might Fergus steadied the weapon and placed the sights on target well within good range. Just as he squeezed the trigger, a tank round slammed into the left side of the vehicle. Shrapnel peppered his right side blasting searing pain up his body. Then nothing...

As the moments passed, the silence soon warmed up to a high pitched whine. His vision went from a black nothing to blurry, and everything slowed down as he began to lose consciousness.

Fergus loved the smell of the night and the burning of wood in the bonfire. Even in the cold winters of Irland. The Scotch helped to ward off the cold along with the warmth of his lady. The two sat on a large wicker chaise longue covered in various animal furs that Fergus trapped. They both sipped gratuitously off homemade Scotch and enjoyed the fire and warmth of each other's bodies.

"I love you Fergie!" Helen, Fergus's sexy little wife, said as she was batting her beautiful, sleepy, bedroom eyes.

"Aww, I love you too Lover! I love you more than anything!" Fergus replied.

Helen, cuddling in his lap, jumped up and looked Fergus deep in his eyes. She then began rubbing his chest and cooing.

"How about you take me right here and show me just how much you love me." Helen whispered seductively.

"Oye! That is a grand idea love!" Fergus replied with a huge smile. Grasping her little waist, Fergus effortlessly lifted her up and placed her standing on the Chaise longue they were sitting on. She was a petite woman and could look Fergus eye to eye now. She let out a cute giggle and wrapped her arms around him.

"Hmmm, make me scream lover!" she whispered. Fergus grabbed the scruff of his animal fur robe and flung it off. There he stood naked in front of Helen, who most certainly approved. Fergus then grabbed Helen's robe ready to rip it off her little body when she suddenly stopped him and placed her hands on his cheeks, pulling him close.

"Fergus! Shoot the fucking rocket now!" she yelled.

Confused Fergus looked around.

"Um... Not to spoil the mood Lover but there are a few more steps to this process before any rockets are *fired*" He replied.

"God Damnit! Fire the fucking rocket you God damn Paddy!" she yelled again and then slapped him across the face.

He took a deep breath as his body and mind tried desperately to recover. Just at that moment, his vision blurred and then filled with bright lights trailing into nothing. Everything slowed to a crawl.

For a moment, nothing seemed real. Fergus just felt like he was floating... dizzily. He knew he had to do something, but he couldn't remember what the hell it was. The pain subsided, and he looked around for clues as to where he was and what was going on around him. He squinted in confusion. There was a lot of commotion, and it was hard to tell what it all meant.

"Oooooohhhhh..... sssshhhhiiiittt....."

Fergus could hear Joe far far away and tried to look for him but couldn't find him. Then he suddenly felt something in his hands.

"Bbbblllooooddddyyy..... hhhhheeelll... iiiissss... ttthhhiiissss....?!?!"

It suddenly dawned on him just at that moment that he was holding a rocket launcher. Not only that but he was also hanging out of a speeding truck that was partially on fire. Then searing pain. It all started to come back. All at once! Like a kick in the face!

"FIRE THE FUCKING ROCKETS!" Joe yelled for the umpteenth time.

Fire, wind, noise, searing pain, dirt blasting his face...

"FIRE!!!"

Fergus lifted the weapon and placed the sights on the tank and with every ounce of conviction in his soul, he cinched his body tight to steady the weapon. They were falling apart quick, and he was not going to lose this shot.

The weapon seemed to explode in his hand as the rocket blasted out of the tube. Ten meters in front of him he heard a loud 'thunk' as the missile's engines ignite launching the explosive device to its target.

Time slowed to a crawl... Everyone stopped what they were doing for just a moment and gauged the round as it spiraled down its fraught path. Fergus let the empty shell of a weapon fall from his hand slowly.

He took a deep breath and yelled.

"Goooooooooo!!"

The AT4 round sailed through the air in a slight spiral. It's engines screaming at full power. Joe knew that if the tank was anything like it was in WWII the round would leave nothing recognizable of that once powerful machine.

100 meters from the tank Fergus let out another mighty war cry for the end of his foe.

50 meters he tensed his fist and gritted his teeth as hard as he could in an attempt to help the round psychically to its intended target. Their last hope to get out of the impending death falling upon them that they so surprisingly found.

Then, with a fiery shockwave of destruction, the round impacted... just in front of the tank.

"What the…. FUCK!" Fergus turned around and began slamming his fists on top of the truck like an angry gorilla on crack.

He was going to start frantically yelling in frustration but stopped when he noticed they were entering a tunnel.

"Oh hey… We win!" Fergus denounced while bleeding profusely from the face and shoulder.

"Hit the brakes!" Joe commanded.

All four vehicles came to a screeching halt slamming into one and other like a train that just derailed. Once they settled, however, everyone jumped out cursing and yelling.

"Grab weapons and ammo, leave everything else."

"We got wounded!" Lilith yelled.

"Get them in the lead vehicle and dump all that crap in it too!" Joe shouted as he sized up what vehicles he had left. Number two was down and already half engulfed in flames, and number four was a total loss with four wounded crawling out. Joe just stood there in awe that they were able to stop at all.

Shaking it off, Joe turned and rummaged through a small black case, pulled out four White Phosphorus Grenades tossed the case aside. He then yanked the pins and chucking the grenades out one by one into the abandoned vehicles.

"Let's get the fuck out of here!" He commanded.

Audible pops sounded from the abandoned vehicle. Then a second later they started to light up like a continuous lightning bolt flashed inside as the phosphorus ignited.

Everyone saw what Joe did and double timed it to the only two vehicles left, jumped in and tore off as fast as they could.

"What do we got Jack?!"

Jack shouted from the very back of the truck.

"Four ambulatory, two priority and one surgical. Wess has two large caliber wounds to the upper thigh and is bleeding profusely. I think I can get it under control as long, and the Femoral wasn't hit."

"We are not going to make Strategic Command. We are compromised! Can you stabilize him!?"

"I'll try Joe."

Lilith moved to the very back with Jack and began working on Wess. She squeezed into the cargo area, leaned up against the wall of the truck and pulled Wess in between her legs with his back to her chest. He was in severe pain and was trying to hold on as best he could.

"I got you Wess. I got you!" Lilith held him tight, trying to calm him down. Wess grabbed onto her like a scared kid and began sobbing uncontrollably as Jack quickly put a tourniquet on his leg.

Once the tourniquet was secure, Jack checked his other wounds. Wess had injuries everywhere as Jack tried to find the worst to work on, but there were too many. Lilith and Jack locked gaze and in that instant had a whole conversation without saying a word. Wess was in severe trouble.

"Knife! ICB Bandage!" Jack shouted as they began ripping Wess's pant leg open.

"Rope!" Lilith cried a half moment later. Fergus handed her a length of half inch line as they hurriedly pulled out several ICB bandages and readied them for use. Lilith fashioned Wess a Bite for the pain, Jason and Mike turned around, and each grabbed Wess's hands. They tried talking to him as best they could, attempting to turn his focus from what was about to happen. Wess knew what was going on, and he knew it was a last ditch effort to save his life. Everyone else just sat and held their breath. Wess's screams were almost unbearable to the crew but when Jack opened up the wound with the knife and jammed the ICB bandages in... Wess's cries became nightmarish.

Then suddenly the horror stopped. Seconds rolled by with only the big V-8 roaring in the background.

"JACK!" Joe shouted breaking the silence.

"I.. ah, I think he passed out." Jack returned.

Jason began slapping Wess in the face calling for him to respond... nothing. He slapped him again. Harder out of desperation.

"He's in shock...! IV!" Jack shouted.

"No, it'll thin his blood! He'll bleed out!" Jason responded.

Jack turned to Jason and with a calm voice and a solemn expression on his face responded.

"There's nothing left to bleed out. This is Wess's only shot."

Jason on the verge of falling apart looked down and noticed Lilith and Jack were wading in a pool of blood. All from Wess.

"Fuck!"

Fergus and Mike were already passing IV bags and tubes up and began reading tape for the procedure.

Markus called up from the rear truck to Joe over the radio in a panic.

"Joe... What the hell is going on up there? There's fucking blood leaking out of your truck. It's getting difficult to see! Is everything OK?"

"No, Take the lead!" Joe stated emotionless.

"Shit! Taking the lead!" Markus cursed. He knew something was horribly wrong.

The second truck quickly overcame Joe's truck and took the lead. Everyone in Truck 2 tried to see what was going on but couldn't make out who was in the back or who bleeding out.

Jack, not worrying about infection, thrust the 18 gauge needle into Wess's arm, plugged him in and opened the IV at full bolus. Jack then repeated the procedure with the other arm.

Lilith, checking pulse, looked at Jack and shook her head.

"DEFIB!" Jack shouted.

"It's in the other truck…" Lilith answered calmly as she laid Wess's head against her shoulder. Cheek to cheek she began stroking his hair.

"You did well Wess…" still locked with Jack's gaze.

Jack just sat there shaking his head.

For the rest of the trip Lilith held Wess tight and comforted him as best she could… stroking his hair, kissing his cheek and telling him it was ok. Jason, stunned and holding back tears, never let go of his friend's hand either.

CHAPTER 5
"Buds."

Las Vegas, Metro County Jail, holding cell eight, earlier that day.

Val and Monty were the best of friends and completely addicted to their trade. Special Operations was on their minds twenty-four hours a day seven days a week. That and girls...and beer...porn might be there a lot too. Even on their off time they always found something that would get them in deep trouble. With endless energy and a childlike vision of right and wrong, these guys were always in trouble.

Val was a huge Russian Spaznautz assigned to the unit as a special weapons and explosives expert, and Monty stood a thick five foot five. He was an expert Brazilian Ju Jitsu fighter and jungle warfare expert. The oddest couple you have ever met. The team loved them though, announcing them as the "Master Blaster" team. It made them proud to attain such a title. Joe, on the other hand, appreciated the skills they brought to the team and their constant need to do good guys shit. The problem with them, however, is that they would always get themselves in trouble and Joe would always get them out. And Joe was getting tired of it.

"Joe gonna kill us." Val stated re-adjusting his nose.

"Aye Dios Mio! I know." Monty blurted.

The two just wanted to spend four days in Vegas, and party like there was no tomorrow. Unfortunately, after the fifth day, they ended up clashing with the Los Vegas mob over a rather "healthy' blond... Who loved the attention.

"Did she give you her number brother?" Val inquired

" Si... but nobody at the construction company knows who I'm talking about. At least we killed some mobsters dude!"

"Ha Ha Ha! You always make me feel better brother! But what are we going to do about these unsavory types staring us down?" Val stated referring to the large group who decided they needed to "Orient, " the newbies to the yard.

"I'll be Jacky Chan yo, and you will be Ivan Drago from Rocky!"

"I like that game."

Such talk never ended well.

Two days later...

Because of the riots Val and Monty started they ended up spending the last two days in isolation. Their six by fourteen-foot cement rooms were adorned with a stainless-steel sink, toilet, and a thin mattress on a cement slab for a bed. The door had a small six inch high by eight inch wide double pained safety class window with a tray slot just under it for meals. One forty-watt bulb surrounded by an industrial steel tubing immersed the room is a sick, pale light. The walls were painted in a green sea foam color that only made the room more uncomfortable.

It wasn't supposed to be a comfortable stay here, but nobody told Monty or Val that. Buds till the end they communicated via Mores Code through the wall separating their cells. Talking outright would only get them placed in separate blocks making isolation not so much fun. Most conversations involved booze or boobs, sometimes guns. But tonight, the conversation made a turn. How were they going to get out of this one? About an hour after lights out Monty posed the question.

"*Dude, I'm kinda worried.*" Monty tapped.

"*Joe will find way. He always do.*" Val replied.

"*Dude. Funny. You tap with a Russian accent.*" Monty joked.

"*And you tap like surfer... Dude.*" Risking being heard Monty whispered aloud.

"Fucker!" Monty tried to think of something clever to reply when the lights suddenly came on. Both men winced at the brightness while shielding their eyes with their hands.

"What the Fuck bro?" Monty blurted out loudly.

"They cannot blame this on us this time, no?" In the distance, Monty and Val heard men yelling. Monty figured it to be another riot and moved to the tray slot and opened it.

A barrage of gunfire could be heard from deep in the prison. Val was sure he could distinctly hear dozens of fire teams assaulting the prison.

"That is not typical Monty. Correctional officers only have shotguns. That sounds like an assault!" Val stated.

"Yeah, that's not okay. My spider sense is tingling! Bro we need to get out. If the other prisoners get here, we are enudo."

"Monty my friend... if I knew a way out, we would be out." Val whispered through the slot.

Suddenly the lights flickered just a bit.

"That's no-Bueno bro..."

The lights stopped flickering... then suddenly became brighter than they should be. An electrical whine then emerged from the silence and quickly became too much for Val and Monty to handle as they grimaced in pain and covered their ears with their hands.

"WHAT THE FUCK BRO!!!" Monty yelled.

No sooner did Monty finish yelling the forty watt bulbs in all the cells in the whole block began exploding one be one. Most of the halogen lights in the hall did the same except a couple. Those that survived began to flicker intermittently. Then suddenly a shockwave slammed through the block as if an airliner crashed into the prison. Dust and debris fell from the ceiling, and as if nothing happened there was silence.

"Oh shit!" Monty whispered.

Val and Monty just froze in place kneeling on the ground and still grimacing not sure what to do next. Then, without warning, all the doors in the block unlocked simultaneously. Val and Monty's expressions went from grimacing to blank instantly. Both completely unsure if the now unlocked doors were a good thing or not. They both took a second to think about their situation. They can get out... but then again... something else can get in as well.

A mixture of shotgun and automatic gunfire could be heard emerging from deep inside the prison. "Those gunshots are inside the prison bro!" Monty whispered. Both figured the shotgun fire was from the guards but couldn't figure out who was shooting the automatics.

"Dude that's not friendly auto fire." Monty whispered in the slot at the door.

"We should leave now. Something tells me Joe needs us." Val and Monty slowly opened the doors to their cells and peeked out. Suspiciously and slowly they surveyed the area. All the doors were unlocked and ajar, but the door at the end of the block was wide open. Val and Monty both looked at each other and shrugged their shoulders. Val gave Monty a head nod, and the two began to creep out of their cells. No sooner did they get ten feet something huge lumbered by the cell blocks entrance. Val and Monty couldn't quite make out what the thing was as they squinted and blinked in the flickering lights. Then suddenly the lights came on for longer than a second and both men frozen in horror as to what they saw.

The thing stood a little taller than a man and weighed about four hundred pounds. Its skin was pale covered in blood and hung loosely on the overdeveloped muscular body. Its head was more like a skull with a thin layer of flesh. It had no eyelids, and its eyes were bone white like two eggs shoved in its head. Jagged teeth hung from its lipless upper jaw as its lower jaw composed of multiple double chins and jiggled grotesquely as it stumbled around. Ripped down the middle of its face where its mouth should have been was a grotesque gaping hole. It labored as it heaved air in and out of this gaping hole of a mouth coughing spittle as it did.

Val and Monty instinctively sprawled to the ground in an attempt avoid its detection. The beast continued, lumbering slowly past the door, almost as if it was blind and following its huge eight-foot gnarled tongue that probed the hall as it moved. Soon it past the open block door and continued down the hallway. Val and Monty slowly moved to their feet and skirted the wall when abruptly the creature grunted. It grunted as if it had found something and began slowly turning around in the hallway. Both men froze in place.

More gunfire, yelling, and screaming came from outside the block but this time louder. The gunfire within the prison was relentless and brutal. It seemed as if the unknown assailant's mission was to kill everything they possibly could. The massacre was getting closer, and both Val and Monty started to become anxious. Their hearts pounded in their chests like pistons on a motor.

Noticing the creature was coming back, Monty turned around and pushed Val back down the hall. Val grimaced in fear and tiptoed away as quickly as he could.

"shit… shit… shit…" Monty whispered under his breath. The two men then turned and went into the nearest room to them and slowly closed the door just enough as to not relock it.

They needed a place to hide. Unfortunately, it is almost impossible in prison to find an opportunistic hiding place.

The light outside flicked showing the two men that they were out of luck with a hiding place. The room didn't provide a place to hide. They couldn't fit under the bunk or behind the toilet. Monty grabbed Val by the collar with both hands and pulled him in and looked him in the eye. His face filled with fear and anxiety. With a squeaky whispering voice, he said something Val couldn't understand. Val just pursed his lip and shrugged his shoulders in response.

Suddenly the two realized the creature was in the hallway about two doors down swinging doors open apparently looking for them. Holding each other by the scruff of their collars, the two stared out the small window in the door in horror. The lights in the hall flickered on and off from multiple directions up and down the corridor. Now and then a little spark floated from the ceiling passing the window.

"shit… shit… shit…" Monty continued again.

Suddenly the light above them pulsed a weak glow, and both men looked up. Then quickly at the door. They then both looked to the casing mounted around the door. It had a two-inch lip protruding from the wall. Both men then looked at each other and pointed to the lip with big smiles on their faces. Just as they moved to the door, however, the beasts head could be seen through the small window and just a few feet outside the door. They both paused but knew they had no more time.

Using the bunk slab as a step, the two men helped each other up to the casing of the door. They then wedged themselves on the casing lip and the steel framing of the ceiling light.

The creature slammed the door open and slowly moved inside. Its tongue slinked about its face tasting the air. As the seconds went by the creature became more and more excited. It seemed it had found what it was looking for and both Val and Monty feared it was them. It began reaching about like a blind man who lost a something valuable. It grunted and groaned at its new choir and started to become angrier and angrier. It seemed to know they were there but became frustrated that it couldn't find them. Its tongue slithered farther out or the gaping hole in its throat and began flailing about desperately.

When thing couldn't get worse, the steel cage of the ceiling light shifted slightly. Fearful to move too much both men looked at the light with just their eyes and saw that the concrete around the fixture was crumbling and the light was coming out of the ceiling. Small graduals of dust floated down along with the deteriorated cement onto the head of the creature.

"shit... shit... shit..."

The creature suddenly paused. A gurgling sound could be heard coming from its throat as it became aware of its surroundings and where its prey is. Its enormous toothed tongue began to slowly slither above its head as it continued tasting the air. Its tongue slid back and forth slowly as it closed in on Monty's hand as Monty looked on in horror. Then the tongue suddenly stopped an inch from Monty's hand, and the beast began to laugh as it finally solved its puzzle.

Without warning a dark figure kicked open the door and started shooting the creature in the back with a pistol. It reared around in shock and then launched its tongue across the room like water from a fire hose. The end of its tongue wrapped around the dark figures head as it screamed. Then, with a mighty yank, the creature ripped the head off the black figure as its cries ceased instantly. Black fluid shot up and splattered on Val and Monty. Then, without a pause, another ominous figured entered the room

"Sterben Arschloch!" It yelled as it unleashed a relentless volley of automatic gunfire from a heavy belt-fed weapon. Bolts of Fire blasted Val and Monty as the attack continued for what seemed to last forever. The creature squealed loudly at first then slumped in the corner and died in a bloody mess.

The dark figure released the trigger and gazed at its accomplishment for a moment. As it tilted its head inquisitively, the metal enclosure protecting the light in the ceiling finally gave way, and both Val and Monty came crashing down landing on the dark figure.

With a thud, the three hit the floor and scurried desperately to gain control of the belt fed weapon. Blood from the tongued creature splattered and sprayed everywhere as the brawl intensified.

Val grabbed the barrel and the stock of the weapon and pulled it in tight to his chest and rolled to his back in between the wall and the first dark figure securing the weapon. Monty jumped on its back and put the thing in a choke hold.

"Sleepy time Chica!" Monty grunted quietly and synched down with his massive arms.

"Piz`da fucking strong one!" Val grunted back feeling the grip of the thing loosen.

The lights continued to flicker as Val finally got a good look at the figure. Its face was covered in blood. Some of the blood appeared dry, and some still looked fresh and wet. But it seemed to be bleeding a black goo. Its skin was pale almost bleached and held to its face tight making it look like an over-developed skull. Its jaw seemed too large and square for its face as it grimaced from Monty's choke. Its eyes were black with deep blue irises and stared at Val as if it could see his soul. Its teeth were a metal color and its gums black. But its eyes… didn't seem real.

After a moment, its eyes rolled to the back of its head, and it slowly passed out. Val shrimped out from under the thing and while still in Monty's grip grabbed the thing by the back of the head and jaw and broke its neck with a mighty jerk.

"Oh fuck bro! Why did you do that!?! I could feel that in my chest!" Monty scurried to his feet wiping off the imaginary filth from the creature's broken neck off his body.

"Po'shyol'no Hui. That thing is not right!."

"What?!?" Monty yelped.

"Look at it! Look at that! What the fuck Bro!" Val yelled.

Monty jumped up and covered Val's mouth with a bloody hand. Val grimaced at the act but put up with it. He knew he was too loud. Monty shushed Val and removed his hand. Blood dripped from Val's face and mouth as Monty looked on in disgust.

"Papi... I'm soooo sooory!" Monty whispered.

Val just looked at Monty with rage in his eyes. After a moment Val kicked the creature over to its back, and through the flickering lights, Monty could finally see the creature's true form.

"El Diablo es esa cosa!!" Monty blurted out stepping back.

"I know right bro? We need to get the fuck out of here now!" Val muttered wiping off his face.

"Is that a Swastika? What the fuck?!?" Monty blurted out.

Val just stared off into the distance not sure at all what to think.

"Gear up bro!" he finally stated.

Monty and Val grabbed the creature's weapons and headed out the door in a tactical manner. Val had the MG42 with a belt of about fifty rounds, and Monty grabbed a Mauser C96 pistol with two magazines.

"We need more guns bro!" Monty whispered.

"We need more ammo to bro." Val replied.

Val and Monty moved into the blocks hallway and made their way to the end of the hall. The door there was open and ajar like most in the block. Monty peered out and glanced into the general area of the block. All three floors opened into a common area with all the general population cells facing each other with a large foyer in the middle. High in the chamber phosphorus lights sputtered on and off intermittently making scanning the area difficult. Men could be heard shouting along with gunfire in the distance.

Monty held up three fingers and started counting down letting Val know they area appeared clear. On the count of three, the two swiftly and silently moved to the walkway outside the solitary cell block. The walkway was made of a steel grate with steel piping for the railing. Several guards and hundreds of inmates laid dead randomly about the entire area. Most died of what appeared to be gunshot wounds, and some were mutilated in an unknown manner. Blood and body parts scattered about almost covering the entire walkway.

The two men looked around in amazement.

"Eto piz`dets!" Val sputtered

"Yeah bro... really fucked up." Monty stated and then tapped Val on the arm signaling him to move out. Trying to stay focused amidst the onslaught of bodies and gore the two moved with great tactical efficiency to the end of the block opposite the control tower. There must have been a fire somewhere in the prison as smoke started filtering out through the ventilation system making it difficult to see.

Val and Monty opened up the emergency exit door and stepped out onto the fire escape platform. It was still and misty out, and the cool fresh air felt good in their lungs. From there just fifty meters up the road a platoon sized element held about seventy inmates and about twenty guards at gunpoint. Val noticed something and pointed to a guidon barrier.

"Is that... " Monty started, but it was only obvious.

There on the guidon was the distinctive insignia of the Nazi SS. Monty then looked closer and noticed most of the Nazi Troopers wrapped in leather and heavily armored from head to toe with masks or faceplates covering their faces. Most walked oddly, with a beastly lumber but with agility. They were fast if they wanted to be.

The Nazi Troopers lined up the group that they had captured two by two on one side of the road. The Troopers then lined up on the opposing side as both began walking down the street. Once the formation was formed correctly, the unit leader halted everyone in the formation. Monty and Val had seen this before, and both men's hearts jolted when they realized what was about to happen. Their minds raced in an attempt to stop it, but it was too late.

The commander in a calm German voice gave the command. It was subtle as if nothing was wrong. Nobody but the Troopers and both Val and Monty knew. As calmly as can be the other Troopers turned, raised their weapons, and shot the inmates and guards point blank. From beginning to end it only took about a few seconds.

"Motherfuckers!" Monty voiced.

Val raised his weapon and without hesitation unleashed a hail of gunfire on the executing squad. In the open and unable to run for cover Val killed most of them to include the commander. Who, by the way, died first.

"Fuck Yeah Baby!" Monty shouted with arms raised over his head.

"That's what you get mother fuckers!"

Other squads of Trooper in the area began to return fire in random directions reacting almost instinctively.

Val knew he had opened up a world of shit, but he didn't care. None of those men, good or bad, deserved to die as they did. He grabbed Monty's arm and pulled him back inside.

"OK! It's game time Monty. They know we are here!"

"Let's do this shit!" Monty yelled holding up is little .38 caliber pistol.

"Yeah, that's not going to work..." Monty put the gun in his pocket and began looking around for another weapon.

"Help me, Bro!" Monty asked, and Val shrugged his shoulders and joined in on the search.

Not a moment later bullets began raining down from the other side of the block. Val and Monty sprinted across the platform to a stairwell and darted inside. Rounds impacted the reinforced metal door with a sonic popping sound as the hit showering sparks and shrapnel in all directions.

"FUCKING MOVE CABRON!" Monty yelled.

Two guards laid slain at the bottom of the stairwell. Each of them with a shotgun. Monty grabbed the one and conducted quick functions check. Once satisfied he grabbed all the rounds he could find and shoved them in his pockets.

"Most of these are non-lethal bro!" Monty uttered

Suddenly the guard's eyes opened and stared at Monty with yellow lizard-like eyes.

"Do what you can Monty!" Val yelled and held up his three fingers but Monty, not saying a word headed out the door dragging Val with him. They were immediately hit with a volley of indiscriminate fire from several Troopers in the hall. Rounds impacted all about them, but the metal grating supplied enough protection till they got to the control tower. Bursting through the door like bulls the two men started to methodically clear the lower roundabout with machinelike precision, only to come under automatic gunfire from several more Troopers above the scaffolding. Instinctively they both hit the deck sprawling as low as they could go. But something wasn't right. Both men looked up and notice about eight Troopers in the control room firing into the bullet resistant glass. They soon realized that the rounds were not penetrating and ceased fire.

Monty started laughing and held up his middle fingers with both hands.

"Yeah, Cabron! That's right! We are coming for you!"

The Troopers became agitated and fired at Monty as he bounced around like a clown laughing at them. Val tried several times to get Monty to go, but he kept taunting the Troops again and again.

"It only bullet resistant Monty. Come on bro! Time to go!"

But Monty was having too much fun and continued with his clowning around when suddenly a single round pierced the glass and slammed into the wall just behind Monty's head.

"Ok! Time to go!" he stated nonchalantly, and the two sprinted down the hall to the mess hall. Rounds from the Troopers slowly chipped away at the glass creating holes big enough to get the barrels of their weapons through. They attempted to shoot down the hall after Val and Monty as best they could. Rounds ricocheted relentlessly down the corridor. Both men had to go the last few meters at a low crawl. They reached the mess hall door and scurried inside.

"Tupitsa you are Monty!" Val yelled.

"I know right!" Monty replied still laughing.

The two men quickly barricaded the mess hall door and then sprinted to the kitchen. Val found a belt of ammo for his weapon around several dead inmates and swiped it up. As they looked around for a way out more automatic gunfire could be heard from behind them. Both men knew that the Troopers had reached the barricaded door trying to bust through.

"Go! Go! Go!" Val yelled desperately.

"What is going on Val? This is shit Bro! Fucking wrong!" Monty blurted out as they entered the kitchen.

The door at the other end of the kitchen burst open as more leather-shrouded Troopers rushed in firing on Monty. Val moved quickly behind cover and reloaded as Monty dived out of the way screaming hysterically. The Troopers concentrated on Monty hoping to punch through all the stainless steel sinks and tables with their weapons.

Val struggled to reload his weapon. The weapon was ancient, and Val felt it should be in a museum rather than being used to assault a prison. After cursing aloud, He got the feed tray locked and pulled the bolt back. He then spun to his feet and hammered countless rounds into the chest of the Troopers. Within seconds the troopers fell to the ground, dead.

Monty jumped to his feet and retrieved one of the Troopers weapons. But to his dismay, Val accidentally shot it up.

"Damn it, Val!" Monty cursed holding up the two halves of the weapon.

Another Trooper burst into the kitchen and raised his machine gun on Monty who stood there wide-eyed and paralyzed. Just as the Troopers weapon leveled several rounds impacted his head instantly exploded it and showered Monty in blood, flesh, and bone.

"DAMN IT VAL!" Monty shouted.

"I had to take time and aim, so I don't hit Troopers rifle."

Monty began dry heaving and wiping the blood from his face and eyes. Cursing and spitting he slowly reached down and secured a Sturmgewehr 44 and several magazines. He quickly conducted a tactical mag exchange and with a disgruntled look on his face waved Val to the door.

"Motherfucker..."

Shouting could be heard from everywhere. Val and Monty needed a way out.

"Those Putos are coming bro!"

"We must distract them and go to the loading dock. We might find truck there, yes?"

Monty rubbed his stubbly face and stared at the Troopers on the floor. Then he saw something on the Trooper and raised his eyebrows inquisitively.

"Um... What is that?" Monty stated, off subject.

Val looked down at the Troop who lay dead at his feet

"Mace hammer?" he replied.

"It's not a fucking Mace hammer you sick fuck! I think that's an old grenade!"

"Oh! Bada Booooom!" Val emphasized the boom part with his hands as if they were exploding and widening his eyes.

"What are you? twelve?" Monty blurted out.

Val slapped Monty square in the chest with the back of his hand and with an "Ah-ha" look on his face stated...

"Twelve inches in your Mom!"

"Unfucking called for Val! My Mother is a fucking Saint!"

Monty pushed Val out of the way and grabbed the grenade. Just then a barrage of rounds blasted through the door coming from the dining area.

"Shit! Time to go Bro!" Monty shrieked and pushed Val to the loading dock. On the way, both men started turning all the switches to the gas stoves to the HI position as quickly as they could.

When they arrived at the back door leading to the dock, Monty paused and held Val back with his forearm, so Val didn't go busting through it. Slowly he eased the door latch open and carefully opened it a crack and peered out. In the loading dock area, Monty noticed at least forty Troopers laying in wait behind cover. It was only obvious that they were waiting for the two of them to come running out. Then, without warning, somebody yelled out.

"Di sind sie! Feuer!"

Monty saw the Troopers suddenly raise their weapons. Cursing aloud, he slammed the door shut and grabbed Val, who was covering the kitchen unaware of their dire situation.

"Fucking move bro!" Monty yelled and pulled the two of them to the ground. Hundreds of rounds exploded through the wall and the door near them. Val and Monty scurried on all fours away from the disintegrating wall but froze only a few feet away. The Troopers in the dining area burst through the door with weapons blazing and inadvertently walk into the crossfire.

Val and Monty grimaced as an ungodly amount of tracer fire passed through the natural gas vapor cloud they had created. Any second now the place will erupt in fire hot enough to cook them both. Making a hard right, the two scurried into the walk-in fridge. Just at the door, Monty fumbled with the grenade trying to initiate the fuse as hundreds of more tracer rounds streamed in like rabid Hornets. Val not missing a step reached around Monty and pulled the pin located at the bottom of the wooden shaft and yanked. The grenade sparked and fizzed to life. Startled by the sudden activity, Monty semi-juggled the explosive with open palms and shoved the burning device into the central kitchen area like a prissy preteen throwing a ball for the first time. Val pulled Monty into the walk-in freezer by the scruff of his neck and slammed the door shut behind them.

The solid door of the walk-in fridge muffled the gunfire somewhat as the two walked backward vigilantly deeper into the freezer utterly suspended in anticipation. A sickly blue light flickered above them teasing their eyes with intermittent pictures of the freezer entrance.

Hours seemingly passed as the grenades five-second fuse burned away.

The scuffling of about twenty men could be heard just outside the door when suddenly one trooper yelled for them all to halt.

It was quiet for a second then suddenly...

"GRANATE!!"

The entire wall surged as the shockwave blasted through the door frame spewing fire and shrapnel in its wake.

"Let's go Monty!" Val yelled.

Both men sprinted to the mutilated door and forced it open. They then stepped into the kitchen cautiously and quickly surveyed their surroundings. Everyone was dead. At least they were pretty sure they were. Moving quickly and trying not to slip on all the blood and guts they made it to the kitchen door leading into the dining area. Val and Monty busted through the door and began aggressively laying suppressive fire only to be met with minimal resistance. Once the dining area was safe, the two grabbed more ammunition belts and headed for the control tower door.

Sprinting down the hall, they reached the control tower door in no time. As if they had done this a thousand times, Val shot out the lock while Monty took out the hinges. The belt fed large caliber weapons made short work of the heavy door. Monty kicked the door in as Val stepped through and laid suppressive fire up the stairwell killing several troopers coming down to investigate.

Heading through the small foyer area at the bottom of the tower Val and Monty again defeated the hulking door at the other end gaining entrance to the Motorpool. Monty kicked the door in, but this time the two were met by an unusual creature on the other side.

It spun and faced them from about fifteen meters away. Shrieking in protest and it stood upright in an apparent fighting stance.

Its body was covered in smooth black scales, and it was colored like a Coral Snake. It looked reptilian but nothing like a snake. It stood on its arms and stabilized itself with two large paws that accompanied three massive claws. Its legs were considerably smaller than humans and pulled in tight to its lower half which seemed to trail off into a scaley horned tail about ten feet long. Its head squared off with hundreds of toothy spikes protruding in from every angle. Monty could see its mouth clearly as its scaly lipless face looked him up and down. It was covered in blood and flesh from a recent kill, and its lower jaw seemed to split while its inner mouth housed hundreds of glass like fangs. The creature took in a deep breath, opened its mouth wide exposing several more rows of teeth accompanied by two claw-like protrusions on both sides of its mouth. They looked as if they were designed to hold prey as the creature consumed it.

Then, like a blast from a cannon, it let out a horrid shriek. Monty and Val just stood there as the creature's breath blasted their faces with spittle and blood. Monty couldn't help but imagined how this thing could quickly snap through bone and flesh with little effort.

117

Nevertheless, without hesitation, the creature screamed again furiously and sprinted towards Monty and Val.

"Filho da Puta!" Monty yelped leveling his weapon and with an almost uncontrolled jerk pulled the trigger slamming round after round into the fierce creature. But to his surprise, the creatures scaly skin seemed to deflect the shots. Val stepped to the side of Monty and joined in on the onslaught. The creature stopped ten meters from them with its legs held up in a defensive stance covering its face.

Frustrated, Val concentrated on shooting the creature in the head hoping to kill it. The creature reacted instantly. As if by instinct, the creature's mouth pulled into its skull, and then bowed its head presenting a large bony plate on its forehead.

Again, the rounds seemed to do no damage to the bony plate.

Val, thinking quickly, figured its mouth was a soft spot on the creature.

"This way Monty!" Val yelled.

Both Monty and Val kept their weapons on the beast and rushed to their right deeper into Motorpool. As they clumsily negotiated the mutilated bodies of guards and inmates they kept the creature at bay with a consistent volley of automatic gunfire, reloading only when the other was ready.

The creature grunted loudly and jumped into the air towards the two men. As it did, it flipped its tail like a wipe and sprayed gallons of greenish liquid across the garage splattering against an inmate transport bus near missing them both.

The liquid acted as a powerful acid and immediately began eating away at the buses exterior. Both men, shocked at the sight of a melting bus, started sprinting across the Motorpool desperately trying to get out of the creature's way.

But Val was at the ready. He was patiently waiting for one thing. Val wanted the creature to shriek again. He wanted it to expose its FUGLY mouth so that he could get a clear shot and hopefully kill it. But they were running out of room and quickly reaching the other side of the large garage.

"Monty turn and ready weapon!" Val bellowed. Monty did as he was told whimpering quietly to himself in defiance.

When he turned, he notices that the creature was now hanging off the superstructure of the Motorpools ceiling walking towards them as if it was nothing.

"What the fuck is that fucking thing bro!" Monty yelped.

"Get ready Monty! Shoot the mouth when it creams ok?!" Val yelled back.

The creature suddenly whipped its tail again as the two sprinted out of the way. Green goo splattered all over the wall behind them and began burning through it instantly and all the vehicle repair equipment as well.

Just then, Val and Monty finally heard what they were waiting for, the horrid shrieking of the creature. As if programmed by a computer both men stopped on a dime, turned, and fired their weapons as if they were choreographed dancers. Tracer round blasted through the air smashing into the protruding mouth of the beast and down its throat.

Its shrieks instantly turned into gurgling as the creature balled up and fell from the ceiling landing out of side near a pile of tires. There the creature began protesting violently thrashing about throwing hundreds of pounds of equipment in all directions. Dust and smoke rose up from the area masking it from sight.

"Go now!" Val uttered.

Both men turned around and almost immediately ran into a BearCat APC rig.

"Fuck Yeah! I'm driving!" Monty muttered, and the two jumped inside. Val, cursing under his breath, strapped in tight. He hated when Monty drove. Once both men were buckled up, Monty flicked a switch and sat back looking at the dash. Val raised his hands in protest and asked Monty what the fuck he was doing.

"It's a diesel motor Cabron! You gotta let the glow plugs warm..."

Before Monty could finish his sentence, hundreds of rounds slammed into the back of the BearCat from the newly burned hole in the wall of the Motorpool. Both men leaned forward for cover, as Monty immediately started the motor. Slamming the vehicle in drive, Monty nailed the throttle hard. With its large diesel engine, the BearCat made short work of the aluminum roll up door ripping it from its rails as the beast of a truck launched from the motor pool and into the Sally Port. Troopers rushed for cover and opened fire on the vehicle relentlessly. Sparks and fire erupted from everywhere, spider-webbing all the windows on the truck almost instantly.

"I can't fucking see anything bro!" Monty yelled.

"Just fucking go!" Val advised.

With the throttle wide open the truck slammed into the double lined fence line at about sixty. The heavy armored vehicle pulled most of the chain link from the pole but stopped the BearCat only a few meters outside the fence line.

"Reverse! Reverse!"

"Yeah, no shit!"

Slamming the vehicle in reverse Monty rolled straight back in hopes of hitting the fence line in the same spot but his hopes diminished quickly as the sound of the creature from the Motor Pool could be heard shrieking over the gunfire.

"Your Girlfriend is back Monty!"

"Hijo de puta give me goose bumps man!"

Just then, launching from the Motor Pool like a Mac truck the Scaly creature slammed into the side of the BearCat with such force the vehicle began to roll over.

"Rollover! Rollover! Rollover!" Monty yelled turning the car into the roll and slamming the throttle down again. The truck righted itself as Monty began doing donuts in the Sally Port.

"Which way Bro!" The creature started shrieking next to Monty's window letting him know it was close. Then its massive claws began penetrated the armor as if it was paper. The creature reached the driver's side door and tried to rip it off with its powerful legs.

"Shit Val! It's pulling my door off... Fucking do something!"

Without hesitating, Val leaned over Monty and shoved the heavy machine gun in a small crack the creature had made and pulled the trigger. Fire and sparks exploded everywhere in the truck as Monty tried to cover his face screaming at the top of his lungs.

The creature, now receiving automatic gunfire from inside and outside the truck loosened its grip and laid across the side of the vehicle protecting its face with its bony head plate.

Tank fire from outside the fence line blasted a shell just behind the BearCat blowing the wall out to the prison. Brick and rebar shot across the yard killing several troopers inadvertently.

The creature fearing for its life from the tank fire launched off the side of the truck with such force it rolled the truck onto two wheels again. Monty turned into the roll again screaming 'Rollover' and righted the vehicle.

The creature bounded off the edge of the rooftop and directed its attack back to the BearCat. Just then the tank in the distance fired its heavy cannon again striking the creature on the side. It exploded in the air directly over the Sally Port. The tank round vaporized its flesh and blood as it rained down over everything in the general area.

For an instant everything was quiet. No one fired, and no one moved. Everyone was shocked the tank hit the damn thing in mid air. Val and Monty were the only things in the area causing havoc as they continued doing circles in the Sallyport with the mauled BearCat. The truck was in bad shape, and its armor almost defeated. But then hope happened.

The blood of the creature began burning everything it touched. The troopers began screaming as their flesh liquefied and peeled off their bodies. The fence itself began to smoke and deteriorate with a quickness.

"Now Monty head that way!" Val yelled seeing a hole appear big enough for the BearCat.

Monty straightened the vehicle out and drove it through the fence line and into the open road. The tank began firing rounds as the BearCat hauled ass down the road, but couldn't target the fast moving truck.

"Dude what the fuck is going on!? What was that thing!" Monty blurted out. He knew Val didn't know, but he had to get it out. Unfortunately, their nightmare was not over just yet.

Only moments down the road the vehicle's armor plates started falling off, and tire began blowing out one by one, but Monty kept the truck going as fast as it could. They got two miles before it finally rolled to a stop. Val and Monty abandoned the now shell of the truck and started jogging down the road in the darkness of the desert.

"Okhu'el?! This is not good?" Val blurted out

"I know bro. I think Joe needs us. There is now way he doesn't!" Monty answered.

Although the ordeal at the prison only lasted a few hours, the whole thing seemed to last days for both men. Creatures and troopers were not on the list of things to fight this night. They may not have seemed like it in their demeanor or by their overtly confident appearance, but both were confused, and they were scared. Something went horribly wrong, and their team needed them and needed them now.

In the distance, the two could hear heavy diesel motors fire up. Faint but distinct the two friend knew the troopers were mounting up to get them.

"Fuck bro... hear that?! We need a car!" Val urged. Both men then sped up their pace and looked for anything that could help them. The only thing they could see right there before them was the vast expanse of the desert. It was about 2:00 am in the morning and the sun wouldn't be up for a while and searching a dark desert doesn't make a person feel confident. Monty began to pray.

Behind them, a twinkle of light appeared in the far distance. Val turned and saw them but couldn't get an accurate number of vehicles in pursuit.

"I think they are pissed bro! They are coming in Armada!"

"There! Overpass!" Monty shouted.

The two sprinted the last 200 meters and came to an overpass. Sitting under the overpass, off to the side of the road was a Nevada State Police vehicle with his lights and engine off.

"Hey! Police! Help!" Monty shouted, but there was no response. About Twenty meters from the vehicle both Monty and Val slowed to a quick tactical walk, raised weapons to the low ready and split up on both sides of the road. Monty slowed down while Val moved to the other side of the road. As they approached the vehicle, Val stopped and pulled overwatch behind the guard rail as Monty paused waiting for the signal. Once set, Val snapped his fingers letting Monty know it was safe to begin clearing the vehicle and underpass.

Monty swept the car with a quickly and scanned the underside of the overpass. Satisfied there was nothing dangerous in the immediate area Money gave Val the thumbs up. Val then quickly hopped over the guard rail and ran to the vehicle. Monty was standing at the low-ready on the other side of the patrol car waiting for Val. Once Val arrived, he took up Monty's six and covered down the road behind the both of them.

"The keys are not in the car, and the cop is laying face down about ten meters in front of me. I think I see his keys on his belt." Monty reported.

"There is convoy en route from prison about five mikes out. Expect incoming from the tanks and mortar fire soon. Keep a low profile."

"Cover me."

Val moved around the car and set up on the opposite side to pull security on the Policemen. Once set, Val clicked his tongue and Monty moved in slow. He slowly and quietly slung his weapon behind him as he approached tip-toeing. The police officers' feet faced Monty as he moved in beside him. Monty looked at Val who gave him a nod and Monty reached in to check the Police Officers' pulse at his neck. Monty knelt motionless for what seemed like forever. Now and then Val shot a glance down the road to check the convoys progression. He was getting nervous, and so was Monty.

Monty finally stood up and moved a knifed hand across his throat signifying the policeman was dead. He then quickly grabbed his firearm, extra mags and the keys to the patrol car.

"Shit time to move!" Monty stated under his breath quickly running to the cop car.

Both men stood at the doors as Monty fumbled with the keys trying to get the doors to unlock.

"Hurry the fuck up Bro!" Val urged.

Just then Monty heard movement from where the policeman was laying and spun around with his weapon raised.

The policemen Monty had just checked was now moving and was trying to get to his feet. Monty and Val just stood there stunned as they watched the officer slowly and awkwardly stand up. It rubbed its face with both hands moaning and grunting as it did.

"Dude... he was not alive." Monty whispered with wide eyes.

"Then what is he now?" Val queried.

From what Monty could see the officer at one time seemed to have been in great physical shape. Maybe a lifter or a physique model at some point. But now the officer coughed and gagged as it looked around curiously.

"Dude...! You ok...?" Monty asked the officer in a confused voice.

Just down the road, a combination of ten Panzer Wagens, both Half Tracks and eight wheelers along with thirty troopers plowed down the road searching for the two escapees. Smoke and cinder bellowed from the machine's exhaust like erupting volcanoes while leather cladding long coat troopers searched methodically from hatched armor. They weren't far off the Convoy Commander thought as he passed what was left of the BearCat.

Monty looked a Val and shrugged his shoulders. "What do we do?"

"Tap on his shoulder. Maybe he not hears you, yes?" Val responded back.

Monty wanted nothing to do with that. Not after what he saw in prison. Something was wrong, something very very wrong and he was staying away. Then again he couldn't just leave an injured Police Officer here with a convoy of troopers heading down their throats. Quickly Monty looked around, found a small rock and threw it at the officer.

"Chorra I'm talking to you!" He stated, louder this time.

The officer froze stiff when the rock hit him in the leg. Just then a clicking sound could be heard. Then, without warning, it spun around with blinding speed shrieking loudly. Monty jumped back as the officers entire body began to morph right in front of him and Val.

Its face elongated suddenly grotesquely. Val and Money could hear bones fracturing and flesh tearing as the thing quickly transfigured. Its belly distended horrifically fast, bursting the gunbelt and tearing the clothing off its distorting body.

Then, without warning, it took several deep breaths, and with each breath, it disfigured even more. Its abdomen burst, spilling intestine to its feet only to be replaced with hot glowing embers that seemed to appear from nothing. The burning embers filled the abdominal cavity and glowed brighter as the creature breathed. Its skin turned black and its face extended out revealing blackish bones that resemble that of an elk skull. Its limbs doubled in size and turned its hands into hooked claws. It shrieked again, this time vomiting molten rock from its face. The burning putrid liquid leaked out of crevices of its bony face. The transformation only took moments as Val and Monty looked on with horrific amazement.

"HOLY FUCK BATMAN!" Monty screamed as both men immediately began firing into the now transformed creature.

From up the road, the lead convoy vehicle reported the gunfire up ahead and ordered the convoy to open fire. The three lead vehicles formed up three wide on the highway and began firing relentlessly onto overpass with twin mounted MG34's, light artillery and rifles.

Rounds started impacting all around the overpass as tracer rounds blasted by like burning bolts of fire. Val and Monty quickly ran out of ammunition and desperately tried to get into the police car. Monty looked over his shoulder just as the creature leered over him. Now close to fifteen feet tall it reared its head back to attack but was struck by 20-millimeter rounds knocking it to its back. The creature had grown tenfold from its original size with a long black bony tail and a long neck. Its insides smoldered with black smoke and cinder billowing out of its exoskeleton. Breathing around the creature became almost impossible.

The creature leaped to its feet and drew in a deep breath facing towards the convoy. Monty and Val finally were able to scurry into the police vehicle unnoticed. Once inside Monty fumbled with the keys some more.

Just then the creature opened its boney mouth and disgorged a flame hundreds of meters long down the highway. The fiery breath looked more like a jet engine at full throttle then fire and the beast needed its elongated clawed hands and feet to keep from blowing away. The blast rumbled through the ground. Even though Val and Monty were in the police car, the heat from the blast almost became intolerable. Both Monty and Val covered their faces from the assault with their arms.

"Holy shit! Holy shit! Where's the keyhole!" Monty blurted out trying to find the keyhole to start the car while still protecting his face from the heat. His heart sank as he looked out the window realizing that the creature may still have the key somewhere on its dragon-like body.

"It's a push start Monty!" Val yelled as he pushed the start button to start the vehicle, but it wouldn't respond.

The creature stopped, and so did the convoy. It drew another breath as best it could, but the barrage of rounds slowed its progress.

"Why won't it fucking start!" Monty screamed

"Put foot on break!" Val ordered. Both men could feel the doom of the situation sneaking up and were getting fearful that this may indeed be the end of them.

Monty slammed on the break as Val hit the button and the cruise sprang to life just as the creature continued its fiery assault down the road.

Without hesitating, Monty slammed the vehicle into drive and nailed the throttle. The car launched itself forward as Monty quickly steered to the onramp of the overpass and darted down the highway while both men were screaming the entire way.

"We fucking made it Dude! Holy Fuck Me!" Monty gasped.

Val looked behind them and could see the battle ensuing between the creature and the troopers. Colossal pillars of Flames and relentless tracer rounds blasted the area in a spectacular explosion of fury. Val and Monty were in awe at the impressive sight.

Then something caught Val's eye. It was a sign. A sign with an airplane on it indicating the airport was in the other direction.

"Monty stop! We have to go back!" Val ordered

"Back?! Back to what? I don't know if you noticed, but that kinda looks like a Lava and jet fuel vomiting Satanic Dragon beast is battling the 3rd Reich back there... as if that's possible... but issssss possible because it issssss going on like right now... the fuck we are going back bro!" Monty responded in a very sarcastic voice.

"The Airport. It's the other way bro!" Val knew the next airport was at least a couple of hundred miles away from where they were. He also knew that the shit had hit the fan and they needed to leave as soon as possible and find Joe.

"Fuck! Fuck! Ok ok ok!" Monty yelled as he began slowing down.

"Move quick Monty before it gets too bad there!" Val ordered.

"Define too bad... cuz I think it can't get much worse bro!"

Monty nailed the throttle as the vehicle raced back to the overpass.

"Oh, glorioso apóstol San Judas, fiel servidor y amigo de Jesús..." Monty prayed but was interrupted by Val.

"Lights! Turn the lights off!" Val ordered.

"Damn bro how!?"

The two started pulling and pushing switches and buttons randomly. Just as they approached a hundred miles an hour, Monty cursed loudly and pulled all the switches on a control box mounted to the ceiling. As he did the vehicle suddenly came to life with all its lights and sirens blazing away relentlessly.

"No no no fucking Eres Tan estupido como un perro Monty!" Monty cursed to himself, but it was too late. They had reached the overpass.

Time slowed to a crawl... Monty skillfully evades debris, jet flames, and tracer rounds while both men screamed aloud like fangirls at a Menudo concert. Shots blasted through the rear windows and trunk sending metal shards, glass, and sparks flying everywhere in the interior of the patrol car as the creature saturated the entire left side of the patrol car with its fiery breath. Monty could feel the heat of the inferno sear the ends of his hair on his face and scalp. Val could feel the puffs of air smack his face as 20-millimeter rounds strafed his head. Both men at that point came to the conclusion that maybe they should have just kept going straight.
But it was too late.

The force of the barrage acted on the patrol vehicles ability to stay on the road. Just one 20 millimeter round could easily PIT a car let alone ten rounds, and the equivalent of a 747 jet engine at full throttle from the Dragon creature working the patrol car in the other direction didn't help either. By sheer instinct, Monty spun the wheel left and right with great anguish to keep the patrol car on the road.

By the hair on their asses, they made it to the other side of the overpass blasting down the highway like a satellite re-entering the atmosphere and emergency lights and sirens still ablaze the whole way.

Slowly their screams faded out to an embarrassed grimace as Monty reduced the patrol cars speed to about ninety miles per hour. An awkward silence came over the both of them as they both tried to process what just happened.

Val shifted uncomfortably in his seat and finally began messing with the emergency lights and siren control box.

"I guess... I will fix this yes?" he stated.

"Yeah... Yeah, that's a good idea." Monty replied rubbing his head where the hair burnt off.

They drove for countless miles and not once saw anything. No traffic, aircraft flying over, nothing. The sky started to light up announcing the dawn approaching. The sense of hope filled the air for the two men.

Monty saw a sign and pulled off to the side of the road near the fence line. There they found another sign that stated "Nellis Air Force Base."

Once the car came to a complete stop, the engine died immediately. Monty tried several times to start the vehicle, but he knew there was no hope. He was impressed it lasted as long as it did.

The two sat in the vehicle for several minutes staring off into the sunrise. Numb from the night's activities with their bodies drained of energy but too confused to sleep they just sat there. Each took turns trying to say something but couldn't find the words. Confused and tired they needed a boost. After a few moments and unable to put the night into perspective, Monty decided to go a different route.

"An officer walked up to a Soldier and asked the Soldier if he had change for a dollar." Monty's voice burst through the silence like an air horn jolting Val back to reality. Val looked at Monty for a second and began chuckling under his breath shaking his head.

"And then what bro?"

"The soldier said 'Sure buddy!' This angered the officer and asked the soldier if that was any way to address an officer. The officer then looked at the soldier with stern eyes and said 'Now let's try that again Soldier.' The Soldier realized the officer was mad and went immediately to the position of attention. The officer then asked the soldier again if he had changed for a dollar." Monty paused with a big smile on his face and smacked Val in the chest.

"What then happened?" Val laughed.

"The Soldier said... No sir!"

The two laughed hard as they got out of the wrecked patrol car. Val looked around as Monty opened the trunk and looked inside. Whatever was in there didn't survive the onslaught of the night and was almost unrecognizable as equipment.

"Fucking nothing." Monty stated. Not at all surprised at what he found. Val, on the other hand, was able to pull up part of the fence line and waved Monty over. With a little bit of squirming and muscle, the two made it underneath. Brushing themselves off on the other side of the fence, they began surveying the area for danger.

The sun reached the horizon, and the two got their first to look at Nellis Air Force Base in the light. It was in ruin, completely destroyed. Aircraft and buildings smoldered sending columns of smoke into the air.

"Holy shit!" Monty blurted out.

"I know right?!"

"No Bueno Bro! What the fuck happened here?" He continued.

"Over here. We need to focus. We need Trans buddy." Val tried to get Monty focused again. He could tell that the destruction of the US base and the deaths of all those young Airmen and woman took a heavy toll on Monty. But they needed to move.

Val walked towards his buddy and put his hand on his shoulder. Speaking softly Val said,

"Monty... we can't get them back... but we can get even no?" Val said in a calm voice. Monty looked at him with eyes wide with disbelief.

"What is going on Bro?" He asked after a moment.

"Bad shit bro. We need to keep moving." Val stated, but this time he had a little more urgency in his voice.

Monty nodded, and the two moved across the tarmac quick and low, using crashed aircraft and burning debris to conceal their movements. Neither had any ammo but held onto the two empty weapons regardless. At the very least they could use them as bats.

Randomly, ungodly shrieks and roars could be heard all around them. It was more of the creatures, but they couldn't see them or even figure out what direction they were in such a mess. About a hundred meters into the destruction then found several large craters created by what they assumed were bombs dropped to destroy the landing field.

"Dude! This is fucking deep hole man! This shit here is military grade. No HME could pull this off." Monty whispered. Val nodded in agreement then pointed to their left.

"I think I saw two Airmen down just over there. They may have weapons. On three, no?" Val stated and held up three fingers. Monty positioned himself to look over the edge of the crater to check the area out. He then glanced quickly and gave Val a thumbs up. Val counted down from three, and the two pushed out of the crater and headed to the bodies not far away.

They quickly arrived under a downed F15 fighter. It looked as if the fighter was trying to take off but never made more than a few hundred meters from where it was parked. The two Airmen were using the aircraft for cover when several large artillery rounds hit the vehicle. Their bodies were mangled horribly. Black pools of blood pooled all around them. Their weapons laid nest to the in pieces, nonetheless both carried M93

Beretta pistols with one extra mag which Val and Monty quickly secured.

Suddenly, while doing a quick function check of the pistols, the two bodies began to move. Monty taped Val's arm and took a step forward to check on them but was snatched up by Val quickly.

"Remember the fucking Dragon!" he whispered in Monty's ear with great distress in his voice.

Monty froze as if in a panic. Then suddenly the two could hear bones snapping and meat ripping. Still holding each other like an old couple in a crowded mall full of kids the two slowly stepped back.

Unexpectantly, the Airman that was closest to the two men coughed. It then moved its arm as if it was trying to get up. With wide eyes and weapons half-assed covering the creatures, the two started sprinting away to the nearest cover. Monty pulled in Val and started screaming in a whimpering voice at him.

"People keep coming to life as fucking Monsters bro! What the fuck Is going on! This is fucking bullshit!"

Val pointed again to a building not far from the runway. It was an Aircraft hanger used to store museum planes, and it appeared to be undamaged.

"Look, bro, I'm guessing that building may be safe. We can figure out what to do there yes?" Val stated.

It took the two almost an hour to get to the hanger. In and out of burning wreckage and unseen horrific creatures. Val and Monty seemed to notice that as the sun gets higher and brighter, the activity of the creatures appears to slow down. By the time they reached the hanger, there was no sign of anything living… or undead in the area.

Monty and Val laid low for a few hours just trying to see what their options were and to open up an opportunity to escape if possible. The invaders destroyed all the Aircraft during the fight it seemed. All that was left was the museum pieces in the hangar where they were laid up.

Monty has some experience in flying and holds a civilian pilot's license. In a way, he became relieved that none of the military aircraft were operational. He could fly a Cessna with no issues or even a Gulfstream jet. But he had no clue how to even start the engines of a C5 Galaxy of even an F15.

"Ok soooo… I'll check on some of these planes and see if any are even flyable." Monty stated matter of factly.

Val nodded and began securing the area.

"I will keep a look out… and try to find a radio yes?"

Monty examined several smaller aircraft and found that most were just gutted display pieces. But out of curiosity, he decided to board an old B17 Fly Fortress. This bomber was one of the most beautiful aircraft he has ever seen. Huge, sleek, powerful and not to mention it carried a bit of World War II nostalgia with it. A true symbol of American industrialism and firepower.

Boarding the aircraft, Monty immediately found himself in awe at the awesomeness of the old bomber. He then found himself at one of the side door gunner positions and began making shooting noises as he pretended to shoot down Luftwaffe fighter planes. His child-like act, however, was short-lived when he notice Val staring at him from across the hanger disapprovingly.

Monty put his hands up as if to say he was sorry and moved up to the aircraft's pilot seat. The controls seemed simple enough as Monty began flipping random switches and pulling toggles. Suddenly the Aircraft came to life. Hydraulic systems started pumping, and dials sprang to life. It didn't take long for him to figure out that this aircraft was ready to roll.

"Ooooohhhhh Sssshhhiiitttt yyyyeaaahh!" Monty sang like a little kid finding his dad's porn stash. He immediately jumped out of the seat and ran to find Val

"Dude! Dude! I got one! And its tanks are full!" Monty blurted with excitement.

"Ok, I was thinking that maybe we can quietly push the plane out and clear us a field like nearby. Maybe a road of something yes." Val stated.

"Um yeah... No! Like it's going to be a combat takeoff like we did in Afganistan. You know... like full throttle and balls to the wall. Right?"

"Monty that is not good idea. It is calm now which means we do not know where the enemy is. We need only to make noise when last resort ok?"

"Ok.. yeah good plan. But one problem." Monty added

"What Monty?"

"The Aircraft is like... Well... A bomber!" Monty sprung the bomber word out like it was a cute surprise and then quickly corrected himself and added that it was a B17 bomber.

"Monty please... no... we can't push... that is too big." Val protested.

"Buddy look..." Monty pulled Val to the hangar door. The aircraft pointed towards the street leading up to the Museum hanger, and the road leading away ran straight to the cantonment area and into the open desert.

"We just roll up the door quietly and turn the engines on and then make a left just out of the parking lot. Bust down that road there and boom! We are airborne. It also has modern coms so we can call Joe and the other. No problem see?" Monty explained.

"Monty this is not good idea. Maybe we can get car instead or helicopter yes." Val pleaded.

"Look, Val, this thing can fly anywhere in the country on one tank of gas. A car can't do that, and I don't know how to fly a helicopter. Plus it would be Bad Ass to this thing bro! She's a beast! Look at the Nose Art!" Monty pointed to the nose of the B17 bomber. There in big black and red letters read the words "Long Range Lilith" and a picture of a woman with long flowing red hair in a skimpy flight suit and high heels.

"Mother of God!" Val yelled out loud uncontrollably.

"I know right!" Monty added almost proud of his find. Val placed his hands on his face and forcedly tried to rub the stress out of his mind.

"Ok but can you get over the curbs and what about the light poles?" Val asked concerned.

"C'mon Val. It's me I can get around that stuff easy. Look there's plenty of room." Monty motioned to the road and tried to look as confident as possible. He had no idea if he could, but he was just happy they were going to try.

"Now let's go get some crew served weapons systems to arm up this bitch!" Monty stated quickly changing the subject and bolted off to the other side of the hanger.

Val just shook his head and moaned under his breath. Within several hours they had acquired four M240Bs and one M2. Surprisingly the M2 .50 cal fit perfectly in the front nose cone of the bomber but the M240's need some help locking down. Before they knew it, the sun was going down.

"Monty look. We only have about 20 minutes, and the sun will be down. We have to go now yes?!" Val stated.

"Ok ok... get the roll up door, and I will prep the motors." Monty then jumped aboard the bomber and began priming the four massive engines but ensured they didn't start till Val was on board.

The roll up doors were motorized and entirely too heavy to roll up by hand. The noise they would make wouldn't subside till the doors were all the way up. Val knew that it was game on as soon as he hit the button. He took a deep breath and then jammed the button with a screwdriver jamming it down. The electric motors sprang to life and pulled the slack in the doors metal slats making a surprising loud clatter. This clattering racket continued as the heavy door raised in a painfully slow manner.

Satisfied the giant door would open on its own Val darted off under the bomber and removed the chock blocks from the wheels tossing them carelessly off to the side. Val looked around quickly and scanned the darkening hanger. Groaning loudly, he boarded the aircraft and closed the door behind him.

"We are prepared Monty! Get us the fuck out of here!" Val yelled as he ran to the Cockpit.

Monty began clicking the engines over one by one as the hanger door reached the halfway point. The process was painfully slow, and even Monty started to feel that this was a bad idea. After several minutes the number one engine cracked over and stalled out.

"Monty! What the fuck! Just turn them all on at the same time!" Val ordered feeling the anxiety rising in his chest.

"You can only start one at a time Val, Dammit!" Monty screamed at Val.

Just then the roll-up door reached the top with a loud clash of metal, and for an instant all was quiet. There the two sat with the hanger door wide open with the bomber engines silent. When suddenly the motor to the roll-up door began to screech loudly. Both men looked up at the door rig in horror.

"Oh fuck! Did you jam the door button?" Monty asked.

"Yes… why?" Val asked. But it was obvious what he had done.

The housing that held the roll up door gave way as the roll-up door began to rotate free on its axis as the free end of the roll up door came around hundreds of pounds of metal slats flipped over the top of the rollers and swung down slamming into the hanger. The clashing of the metal could be heard for miles. This clashing continued every ten to fifteen seconds as the motor mindlessly rotated.

"Fucking dinner bell bro! Shit!" Monty exclaimed as his heart sank in his chest.

"Start the engines Monty!" Val yelled.

Monty kept priming the motor and got one started. Then another and then another. The whole process took at least ten minutes.

"Let's go now Monty. We should have enough power yes?" Val asked excitedly.

"We Can't! We need the fourth engine started to get over the curbs." Monty answered but was suddenly distracted.

"Did you see that! Something moved! Over there!"

"Fuck!" Val exclaimed and jumped out of the seat and headed to the nose gunner position. Monty kept looking out the door and tried desperately to get the fourth engine started.

Val reached the .50 cal mounted to the nose of the bomber and readied the weapon. Each weapon had about 400 rounds each, and Val figured they could lose all of it in a firefight if need be.

The sun finally sank as the parking lot of the Museum hanger turned an orange color. It was empty of vehicles, but Val still scanned it for anything. Suddenly something caught his eye.

"Scary Little Girl! She's right there! A hundred meters out! Shoot the damn little Girl!" Monty screamed hysterically.

A little girl, covered in blood, slowly floated across the parking lot wearing a onesie pajama. She was suspended in the air as if she was held up from her shoulders, dangling limply with her feet dragging on the ground. Her head laid back distorted as she leered at the bomber with black and yellow eyes that seemed too big for her head.

Chills ran up Vals back as he pushed the butterfly trigger down of the large weapon. Fire and thunder erupted from the M2 as Val walked rounds across the parking lot to the little girl. She began shrieking hystaricly as rounds impacted her little body blowing off her leg and arm. The impact launched her small body back several meters.

Val stopped firing, but the little girl didn't stop moving. Her body convulsed and contorted at the wounds it received. Val just stared in horror as the creature began to change before his eyes.

Monty finally got the fourth engine started and patiently waited a few seconds for the oil pressure to rise before slamming all four engines into full throttle.

Val suddenly realized that they were now headed directly towards the little girl who now seemed to be growing black tentacles at an extreme rate.

Val began firing again and kept shooting until they were safely passed what was left of the little girl. Unsatisfied the creature was dead, Val moved quickly to the door gunners position stumbling as the large aircraft lurched up and over curbs. Swearing loudly, Val threw himself at the door gunner position and grabbed the M240B.

The creature grew with incredible speed and was now almost four hundred pounds of furious black tentacles. The creature perilously tried to snatch up the aircraft wings as it launched down the road. Val fired a hail of automatic gunfire into the creature in an attempt to keep it safely away.

As they passed, however, he felt something through the turbulence of the aircraft and the pounding of the curbs in the parking lot. It felt like a blast of wind through the gunner's door behind him. Then it happened again… and again. In the not so far distance, he heard Monty screaming. With a quick but reluctant glance, Val looked over his should.

Flapping four monstrous black leathery wings was a man-sized creature attempting to fly into the gunner's door. Its legs elongated and heavily clawed tried to reach in and grab Val from behind. It's arms, heavily muscled, split apart and stretched out creating two sets of wings that ripped through the air with such ferocity Val found it difficult to stand his ground. Covering its head was an Iron helmet with thin long bony spikes protruding through holes drilled in it. The helmet draped over its face with only its mouth exposed. It could extend its jaws from its head several feet, and its elongated cylinder like white teeth and red gums snapped shockingly loud when it tried to bite. Without hesitating and screaming uncontrollably, Val swung the M240B around and off its mount blasting the creatures up and down its body relentlessly. The creature shrieked and convulsed violently flailing its wings and clawed legs madly as it tried to resist the searing pain of the 7.62-millimeter rounds. After about seventy or so rounds it finally gave up and flew off like a rocket.

Val then turned his attention to the tentacle creature on the other side and leaned out the window. Although it was giving chase by rolling its massive body flailing its numerous tentacles in protest, it was unable to keep up. Val took in a deep breath and fell to the floor. Glancing out of the other gunner's door, Val could see huge gash marks from the clawed creature all around the frame of the door. He could only imagine what that would felt like if it had gotten ahold of him. The hair on the back of his neck stood on end.

After several minutes Val felt the aircraft rise and become suspended in the air. They have finally taken off and were in the air. Making one final check, Val glanced carefully out the gunner's door for anything that might threaten their flight. Finding nothing, he reloaded and remounted the M240B and moved quickly to the cockpit with Monty.

"See bro! That wasn't so bad right?" Monty stated as if it was nothing.

Val glared at Monty in disbelief. He then pointed down the aircraft where he came from and stuttered awkwardly trying to find the words to describe what had just happened.

"What Bro?! Chill out. Shit!" Monty said looking at Val strangely like he just lost his mind. Val wasn't sure what upset him more. The way Monty looked at him all crazy like or that fact that he fought off to supernatural creatures just fifty feet away and Monty didn't have a clue as to what happened to him.

Thinking about it, he felt it would take too long to explain the situation. Val had a difficult time finding the words even to describe what happened.

"Right Monty. Easy peasy! Fuck it! Where are comms at bro?" Val finally stated.

"You passed it when you came in. just by the stairs near the crawlspace." Monty said holding up a pair of earphones.

"OK... I will let you know when I'm up yes? You should get us as high as you can." Val responded as he turned away. Monty gave Val a thumbs up and turned his attention to the fact that he was flying a B17 bomber. Clapping his hands together once and then flailing his arms he shouted loudly.

"I'm a fucking Bomber Pilot Mother furckers!!" He then saw a brightly lit display box, and some switches to his right near the throttle control and without caution began flicking switches up and down.

"...whats this do..."

CHAPTER 6
"Little House of Horror on the Hill"

Mid-West America.

The mountainous region opened into the high plains. The sky was crystal clear and the sun, still an hour away showed no signs of influx. It was dark... Very dark... Unusually dark. Except for one corner

"Is that the sun?"

"No... It'll come up over there." Joe pointed to the east just right of the convoy.

"So what the hell's that?" Dave asked.

"Nothing good."

The road turned slightly to the left placing the red glow directly in their path.

"Looks like we're about to find out."

"Yep."

Soon the road opened up into a four-lane highway exposing a more open terrain. Still, things didn't seem right.

"Are those bullet holes?" Dave asked

"Yep. A lot too." Joe stopped the vehicle in the middle of the highway and stepped out with a weapon in hand. Dave got out as well and kneeled down several feet from the truck. He ran a bare finger across the holes they found in one of the vehicles abandoned on the side of the road.

"50 Cal. It's everywhere." Dave started moving to the far side of the road where he found several splintered tree stump.

"...and some heavy guns too."

"You think that's interesting come look at this."

Dave walked around the suburban to the left side of the road as he did the rest of the crew exited the vehicles to see what caught Joe's eye. As each stepped up to the railing to survey the scene, their eyes widened in awe. The sun was still behind the crest of the horizon but what ambient light there was gave way to something nobody ever thought they would see.

Spread about an open corn field freshly cut were the carcasses of a great battle. US Army M1 tanks and Bradley fighting vehicles wrecks laid about in what appeared to be a hasty engagement put together poorly and lead badly. Strewn about them were the burnt and beaten bodies of soldiers.

"Jesus Christ..." someone said breaking the silence.

Dave and Lilith sprinted over the railing and drew their sidearm frantically looking for survivors. "You four... get a med bag and follow them. Jack, get on the radio. We're not going any further till we figure out what's going on."

"Moving!"

Everyone responded and engaged in their task. Joe raised his M4 and scanned the field with his optics. The damage was impressive he thought. Real impressive.

"No answer yet but we still could be too far away. All ComSat, Emergency channels and Land Owner Freq's are silent." Jack reported. He walked up a stood next to Joe.

"Last time I saw a one sided fight like this we were on the dealing side." Jack stated as he watched the others jump the railing with med bags in hand chasing after Lilith and Dave.

"They found something." Joe said in a calm voice. Jack watched him move forward and step over the rail. Jack stayed behind reluctantly to watch the trucks.

Joe walked slowly watching his footing. The sun wasn't up just yet, and it was still dark. However, the ambient light was beginning to brighten the horrific scene.

The group finally caught up with Lilith and Dave falling into a wedge formation behind them. Joe took up the center position for command and control. As they slowly moved through the battle space and as the glow of the sun just before the dawn crept up the full impact of the destruction became apparent.

"My God!" Dave gasped.

"I don't think God had anything to do with this..." Lilith added.

At least 20 M1A1 tanks, 30 Bradley's, and a swarm of support vehicles littered the field along with the bodies of over 400 National Guard soldiers. Everything was twisted and mangled, spread across miles of battlefield. The sight was disturbing and became even more so as the sun approached the horizon.

Everyone stopped. Following Lilith, the group approached a large hole. It spanned probably 40 feet across and at least 20 feet deep. At the bottom of the hole, the team found an M1 tank resting on its turret. And to their horror, bounded to the M1's underside and tied to the tracks with chain and cables was a young female soldier. Her clothes were ripped loosely from her body. It was evident she was brutally violated.

"No no no....!" Lilith protested jumped into the hollow blindly and struggled desperately to reach the young girl.

Jack was scanning around his position and felt very uneasy about everything. Things were moving all around him, but almost as if the things moving were invisible. There wasn't a lot of movement but just enough to grab his attentions. His heart began beating faster and faster.

"Joe, give me a couple guys back here would you please." Jack ordered in his throat mic trying to sound at ease.

"Hold one Jack." Joe replied.

That was not what he wanted to hear. Regardless, he continued to hold his ground.

He finished his 5-meter scan around the vehicles and opened up his search area to about 20 meters. Just down the road, he noticed a four-door Honda that appeared to have rolled on the highway and then came to rest on its roof. In it he assumed was a husband and wife couple and their 4-year-old daughter. Although they were dead, they seemed at peace still buckled in for safety. He raised his rifle and peered down the magnified optics. There he could see the entire family suspended in their seats. Broken glass and blood scattered about them. The Airbags deployed and although now deflated obscured the parent's faces. But he could clearly see the little girl. She was a beautiful child with curly long brown hair and a perfect little doll face. If it weren't for the horrific scene about him, he would swear she was asleep.

"What a waste..." he whispered.

Suddenly he heard something rustle to his right. It wasn't loud or heavy, but it was only about 6 feet away. Way too close. Not moving a muscle Jack swiveled his head slowly to see what it was. He heard it again and tensed up. To his right was the highway railing and just on the other side was a large bushel of wild grass. He could see it now with both eyes, and his heart raced as he prepared for the unknown.

It rustled again. Jack blinked. And then again. Jack flicked off the safety of his rifle and readied himself. He had an FN SCAR 17 packing 30 7.62 caliber rounds. On full auto, nothing would survive at this distance. Armored or not, whatever it was will be dead soon. Jack stared intently... and waited.

Suddenly a small bird popped out from the grassy bushel with a beak full of dried grass. It looked at Jack and flew off almost instantly.

Jack let out a deep sigh, and his entire body relaxed. He was sweating profusely and took a quick deep breath to calm himself.

"Fucking bird…" he whispered and clicked back on safe.

Jack then went back to his 20-meter scan. Looking down the optic, Jack found the overturned car and with the family inside. He then found the little girl and continued his scan from there. Checking the area of the car and then the ground in-between the car and him, Jack noticed something move. He quickly zeroed back on the little girl. Nothing.

'But wait…' He thought to himself. The little girl's eyes seemed different. Her eyes are open; Jack thought to himself almost saying the words out loud. His heart skipped a beat and began thumping in his chest like a drum. But were they open before? Jack thought to himself and couldn't remember. There's no way she could be alive. Or maybe she was? He needed to find out and find out quick.

Jack heard something behind him. It sounded like someone's hand slamming on the hood of a car. Maybe about 15 meters away. He spun around quickly into a crouch with weapon raised and flicked off safe. He scanned quickly and saw nothing. Jack then rotated around and raised his weapon again. Looking over his optics Jack range walked towards the Honda and the little girl. With his weapon ready, he paused in the prone by a wrecked truck and re-checked his situation. He scanned left and right and saw nothing but more wrecked vehicles and bodies. He then pulled his weapon in tight and looked through the optics to his target area. What he saw froze him in absolute horror.

There in the car seat staring back at him was the little girl. Her eyes were wide open and desperate as if she saw water for the first time in days after being stranded in the desert. She clutched the car seat straps with a death grip.

"My God..."

Something large moved to Jacks left. He jumped to his feet, and he rotated left with the weapon raised and ready to fire. Then something moved behind him, and he swung his weapon around and took a knee. He quickly scanned left and right and then spun back around again. Nothing.

"What the..." Jack whispered.

Without moving, he slowly rotated his head to the right where the little girl was, his weapon still at the ready. Jack was closer to the vehicle now and standing up he could see through the window at the girl. He then slowly dropped to one knee. He could see the car seat the little girl was in, but he couldn't see the little girl from that angle. Slowly letting go of the front grip with his left-hand keeping is right on the pistol grip, Jack eased himself down to a prone position keeping an eye out for more movement. Once settled he glanced over in the Honda's back seat. There he saw the car seat, but the little girl was not in it.

"Fuck!" Jack blurted out unconsciously and jumped to his feet. His heart was pounding, he was sweating in droves, and his skin crawled. With his rifle at the ready Jack began desperately searching for targets. Something was horribly wrong, and he knew it.

Lilith made it to with young female soldier and grabbed her hand. It was stone cold and lifeless. Something she didn't expect. It was obvious the girl was dead, but Lilith didn't care and in desperation tried to untie her wrists, but the bonds were too tight. She reached back to pull her knife out when she saw the girls hand jerk. Lilith froze suddenly aware that something was wrong.

"I got movement left." Jason whispered in the mic

"Movement right." Mac added.

"Where?" Joe questioned.

"Umm... Not sure." said another

Lilith's heart started pounding signaling the realization of what was about to come. Her world as she knew it was about to end in one quick glance. She lingered for just a moment with a flash memory of a typical past. She reminisced of a memory of a somewhat typical afternoon for her with a big cup of coffee at her warehouse apartment. The bright sun was streaming through her large industrial windows that towered 40 feet up. Her windows faced the east and from her kitchen table could witness the morning sunrise and all its glory every day. But it seems not today, and it seems never again.

Slowly and cautiously she turned her head to the young girls face. There staring back at her emotionless was the dead girl's eyes. They were wrong in every way. It looked as if someone had ripped her eyes out and were staring through them at her. The white part was almost black, and the Iris was silverfish but smaller than it should be. Disturbing and demented.

Without so much as a warning, the young girl surged forward with great violence and ferocity trying to bite Lilith's face. Lilith leaped backward simultaneously palm striking the girl in the shoulder and drawing her sidearm from her chest rig. Panic welled up in her like a shot of electricity. Time slowed to a crawl as she launched herself off the tank backward letting two rounds fly. Her reaction was almost entirely involuntary. Her aim, on the other hand, was spot on. As if in slow motion Lilith could see the two round slam into the forehead of the young girl. Pink mist burst from each entry point and just a millisecond later exploding out the back thrusting the young girls head back against the tanks armored hull. Her head hit the hull like a rotten pumpkin splattering blood and brain matter everywhere. It had begun. Nothing will be the same again.

Every dead body within 300 meters sat straight up and looked in the direction of the two gunshots. Their eyes were the same as the girls. They scanned around as if desperately trying to figure out what was going on. They seemed almost confused.

"Holy Fuck Joe!"

"I see them Dave!"

Everyone had their weapons rise at the ready and were actively closing ranks. Panic was setting in, but they all held their sectors. Joe wasn't sure what just happened, but he was not willing to wait and find out.

Lilith hit the ground at the bottom of the pit with a thud temporally stunning her. She still was hurting from the incident two weeks ago. Lilith rolled to her side and let out a groan and then cussed. When she did all the dead bodies turned their heads to her gowns. They had a look on their face as if they had finally found the answer they were looking for, what they desperately seek. Chills ran up the spines of the team member as they pushed into within 2 meters of each other.

"Dave get her out of there." Joe ordered in a low voice.

Dave just nodded and moved to the pit and leaned over the edge. With an outreached hand Dave motioned for Lilith to move towards him. Still shaken, she moved to Dave's hand and grabbed it with both of hers. Dave then looked around cautiously, anchored a knee and lifted her up slow. As she crested the edge of the pit, Dave pulled her in tight to her surprise. He grabbed a lock of her hair and pulled her head to his face and Dave calmly whispered.

"Guns up... We're in trouble."

Acknowledging what Dave said, Lilith froze for a second and began scanning around. She saw the team in a tight formation just a few meters away. Then as she rolled onto her back, Dave pulled her in close from behind and forced her face cheek to cheek with his. With one hand and pointed straight out and moved her face with the other in the same direction. Lilith focused on his finger and then refocused to where he was pointing. She didn't see it at first, but then suddenly there it was. A soldier, sitting straight up and covered in blood, was staring back at her. He was about 20 meters away, and his eyes were dark and disfigured as the girls were. His mouth was open, and he was breathing as if he was panting. His arms were outstretched to the side as if he was about to get up but he looked unsure if he wanted to. Lilith got the feeling that it was confused or something.

Lilith gasped at the sight and nodded her head in acknowledgment. Dave then released the tight grip on her, and they slowly moved to their feet. Once on her feet she slowly drew her sidearm and transferred to a low ready position. Dave turned back to back and drew his sidearm as well. They both began to side-step cautiously to the team formation. Then suddenly, something caught their eye.

The team was about 5 meters away from an M1 tank on its side. Mitch was covering the tank edge and saw a shadow begin to form from around the corner. It looked human but didn't move right. He could hear its footsteps as if it limped one step and then dragged the other. Slowly the shadow grew bigger and bigger.

"Contact front." He whispered in his throat mic.

Whatever it was it was beginning to crest the corner. Mitch stepped back stunned. It was a Soldier, and he was burned pretty badly, almost his entire body. He also had a massive wound to his side and was dragging his entrails behind him.

"Oh, shhiitt! Joe?" Mitch blurted out.

Just after Mitch spoke, the burned soldier began screaming a gurgly cry. But it was an inhuman scream and shockingly loud. Mitch, startled, took another step back. There was no way this guy was alive he thought but held his fire. Two more Soldiers made it to their feet and began stumbling to the team. Joe then pulled Dave and Lilith into their perimeter and called out for Alpha team to move and Bravo team to cover. As Alpha team moved out slowly trying not to attract too much attention, the inevitable happened.

The burned soldier stumbled towards Mitch and was getting too close. Mitch warned him to stay back. But he knew the "Thing" wasn't going to obey. Blowing off the second warning Mitch heaved up, and front kicked the burned soldier in the chest launching back a good 10 feet. The creature stumbled but stayed standing and as soon as it regained its balance froze suddenly, shook its head then snapped Mitch a look that could have pierced his soul. Rage filled its face and made Mitch's skin crawl.

"Here we go Mother Fucker!" Mitch yelled anticipating the attack. The creature burst out a horrifying screech, and its body seemed to transform. Its face looked more distorted and mangled, and his body appeared to disfigure right before him becoming longer and more insect like. It then, without warning, rushed towards Mitch flailing its arms wildly and bearing its teeth.

Mitch fired on the creature relentlessly until it fell before his feet. It took about 11 rounds from his M4 before the thing finally stopped attacking. It was now curled up in a ball twitching and quivering, bleeding out dark, thick black blood.

All the creatures around them started screeching, as their bodies began to deform as well. Their masses began to increase around the group, scurried about, flailing their arms, and screaming that blood-curdling scream.

Joe didn't care what was going on. All he knew was they were losing the tactical advantage, and they were losing it quickly.

"WEAPONS FREE! BACK TO THE TRUCKS!" Joe shouted. The group then opened fire killing everything they could as fast as they could. Joe and Dave sprinted to the front of the pack and began clearing the way. Joe would walk forward towards the truck rapid firing on anything in the way. Dave watched the rear with one hand on his back signaling to Joe he was ready. Once Joe needed to reload he shouted "Reload!" and Dave quickly took up Joe's position while Joe reloaded. The rest of the group bounded from cover to cover just behind them. They continued this assault all the way back to the trucks cutting through the hordes of creatures like a wrecking ball.

"Joe I'm red on ammo!" Dave shouted

"I am to Dave! Let's get the fuck out of here.

There at the trucks, Joe and Dave ran into Jack, who was on the roof of the lead vehicle rapid firing multiple incoming targets desperately holding his position.

"Joe! We have to leave here now!" Jack shouted as he fired a round into the head of a woman scrambling up the hood of the truck like a rabid spider.

"MOUNT UP!" Joe shouted as everyone sprinted for the vehicles. Once inside some the group scurried for more ammo or changed weapon systems out completely. Then took up a position in which they could support the rest of the group.

Panic and desperation began to take hold of everyone. They shouted, banging against the trucks in a panic trying to get the others to run faster. Creatures ambushed team member at every corner.   Joe and Dave still outside the trucks and out of ammo slung their rifles quickly and transitioned to their side arms. Carefully shooting targets as the last of the group made it to the trucks.

Jack jumped off the roof of the vehicle and fired twice dropping a creature just feet away. He was now out of ammo and transitioned to his pistol. Shooting two more rounds, he jumped in the truck and started it up.

Dave jumped in the driver's seat of the trail vehicle with Fergus by the opening protecting him while he started the truck. Everyone else jumped in and laid massive suppressive fire in all directions. Once both trucks were up Joe gave the clear to move out and took a quick inventory of personal. All nine present and no seriously injured reported up to him. Joe sank in his seat as it creaked under its new load. They were beaten up and extremely low on ammo. The worst part though was that they still had no idea what was going on.

"Jason... Find a hill. Preferably with a house on it. We need to make contact and find out what to do next. The higher, the better. Got it?" Joe then looked forward and then at his weapon. Jason didn't ever respond but instead immediately began looking for the GPS computer to find out where they needed to go.

"Dave... redistribute ammo in your truck and stay close." Joe commanded over the mic.

"Roger." Dave responded. He then turned to everyone in the truck and relayed the information. They all knew what Joe said but listened intently.

Jason leaned forward and spoke into Jacks' ear letting him know that there was a house about ten miles up and that he needed to head south on Highway 63 then East on 66. Jack noted it and sped up. He was aware that a lot could happen in ten miles. Jason and Joe looked at each other and nodded in agreement.

A few miles up the road Dave noticed something.

"Has anyone seen anything since our last little stop?" He said over the mic. Several people come over the mic confirming that their sector was clear.

"Has anyone seen any people? Cars driving around maybe?" Dave said again.
 "Where did everyone go?"

Dave's observation was not at all unnoticed by anyone. They thought it was strange too, but to hear it out loud sent chills up everyone's spines. The sun was up, and it was getting warmer. Today is an odd day altogether, and it was about to get stranger.

The team reached the house and immediately went on the alert. The house was a large Victorian house with a huge wrap around porch and decorative wood pillars. It was a beautiful house... except for the blood covered Ford Pickup impaled into the front door and the half dozen mangled bodies laying about.

Everyone exited the vehicles quickly with guns at the ready. Alpha Team with Joe on point lined up by the trucks and covered the house. Bravo Team lead by Dave ran and secured the perimeter with teams of two. Lilith squeezed her tiny body between Mitch and Markus at the rear of the entry team. Both men were colossal and didn't mind the company but tried very hard not to step on her.

Dave gave the go, and the entry team moved out with a quickness and made an easy entry. Thirty seconds later all fifteen rooms were cleared, and Bravo team was called in to help secure the house. Jack slowly pulled the vehicles up to blockade the front yard along with Mike. Both Jack and Mike tried very hard not to run over the bodies lying about the front yard. Although, if they did, it wouldn't have mattered much since the bodies were mangled beyond recognition. It was as if they were chewed up and spit out. Jack knew they needed a proper burial but time was not on their side. But that was the issue; they didn't have time.

Shaking it off, Jack and Mike got the trucks lined up in a V formation in front of the house to block the road. Jason and Markus unloaded Wess from the truck and moved him to the woods. There they quickly buried him in a shallow grave. It was the best they could do. Jack and Mike looked on providing cover for the quick funeral as they set up a fighting position for the M240B machine gun. Once everything was secured, Joe called everyone into the house.

"What the fuck happened to those people. If they are people?" Mike asked.

"I do not know. All I know is that it is going to get worse before it gets better." Jack answered frankly.

"Yeah... I got that feeling too."

Jack slapped Mike on the back and squeezed his shoulder in a mute attempt to encourage him. They both knew something big was about to happen and that they might not make it out alive.

Jack retrieved the SatCom system and walked in the house. The place was in shambles. Blood, flesh, and debris scattered everywhere.

"What the..." Jack mumbled as he slowly stepped into the living room.

"It's worse upstairs. Like a blender went off up there. So where do you need this stuff?" Dave replied helping Jack with the gear he brought in.

"Oh uh... Upstairs..." Jack stated as the two stared at each other in dismay.

"Really...?" Dave said after an uncomfortable pause.

"Attic...? Jack answered.

"Yeah... Not happening unless you have a full
     bio

suit." Dave said with a serious look.

"Jack you're going to have to get a ladder and set up on the second story back porch ok? And we are not staying here too long, so please hurry. Help him out Dave." Joe said calmly.

Both men nodded in agreement and went outside to look for a ladder.

"Mitch, go help Mike at the trucks. Fergus, Lilith give me a 50 sweep of the perimeter."

"Roger Joe! Come on Lilith get me out of this place!" Fergus grunted. Lilith glanced at Joe and gave him a head nod.

"Jason, Markus... See if you can find anything worth using. Ammo, food, whatever. But stay downstairs. I'm not digging the décor upstairs if you know what I mean." Joe ordered.

"Yes, Joe. We aren't either." Markus replied as they headed for the kitchen.

Jack and Dave found an old wooden ladder in a shed near the house and erected it near the balcony.
"Is this thing safe?" Jack asked.
"Your guess is as good as mine. Paper, rock, scissors?" Dave stated holding his hand out with his fist in it.

"I always lose that game. I'll go. I will have to anyway. This is my SatCom." Jack observed as he looked up the rickety ladder.
"I have your cover..."

Jack slung his SCAR and unholstered his HK USP. He took a deep breath and reluctantly began working his way up the ladder. Dave stepped back about ten feet and trained his rifle on the edge of the

balcony. His mind kept racing as to what might be up there and had to take a second to shake it off. Jack was vulnerable,
and he needed to focus.

Lilith and Markus moved out to the three o'clock position of the house and announced their location over the radio. Dave noted that they were about fifty meters behind him. Both Lilith and Markus took a knee, weapons low and just listened and looked around. After a few seconds, Markus spoke up in a whisper.

"I don't know what was more disturbing. The gnarled bloody spots on the floor where it looked like someone's insides were dug out or the amount of bloody claw marks on the wall… what the fuck is going on little one."

Lilith shook her head and was about to say something when they both heard a distinctive dump about twenty meters away. Markus raised his rifle in the direction of the sound and told Lilith he had it covered. Lilith then put her head down and closed her eyes. Slowly she began shutting her mind down and only focused on the sounds around her. Lilith is patricianly good at this skill. Her ability to focus and isolate sounds and determine their threat level is uncanny.

"There's a car about 10 miles out… they're running from something… Engines about to blow." She whispered.

"Poor fuckers…"

"Cat…" She whispered again pointing to their left.

"Poor fucker…" Markus said again.

Lilith opened her eyes startled and moved in towards Markus. She placed her hand on his shoulder and moved to his ear. She then pointed to where they heard the thumb earlier and whispered softly.

"Something big is eating something just over there…it sounds raw."

Markus's face turned from focused to WTF instantly as chills crawled up his entire body.

Jack sat crouched on the ladder at the crest of the balcony making sure not to expose himself to anything up there. He then glanced at Dave who gave him a thumbs up. Jack then turned to the window just to his left about five meters away and deemed it safe despite the smeared bloody handprints on the glass. Jack then leaned back and straightened his pistol arm towards the balcony. He then slowly peeked over the edge through the bone-white pilings being careful not to expose more than his barrel and his strong eye.

Blood smeared most of the bone white balcony floor, nonetheless, whatever was there, it's gone now. Jack then moved slowly to the railing while covering the French doors to the balcony. The doors were closed, luckily. As he negotiated the palisade, Dave slung his weapon and began up the steps of the latter, but was immediately halted by Jack. He wanted him there instead of on the balcony. Once over the railing, Jack put the SatCom case down and triggered his throat mic.

"Stay there Dave. Once I set up, we can make the call from down there. Joe, I'll be ready in about five minutes."

"Roger" Joe acknowledged.

Jack took a moment and studied the huge blood stains on the floor of the balcony. Blood pooled in two places with a single drag mark connecting them. Jack figured the person was attacked twice brutally and dragged from spot to spot. Bloody hand prints and claw marks proved the victim was overpowered but struggled desperately anyway. Bloody drag mark then trailed inside house bordered by dark red hand prints as the victim fought the whole way.Blood handprints covered the bottom corner of the door as well, and a piece of the trimming was missing. Although the French doors were closed, it was evident, the victim grasped one door and was ripped off as a last ditch effort to escape. Then again, who closed the doors after the attack.

With his 300 Blackout at the low-read and Lilith trailing right behind him Markus cut through the bush with ease and stealth. Lilith guided him by tapping his leg and pointing with her HK USP .45 in the direction of the noise she heard. Lilith had a hard time keeping up with Markus and his long strides. Every few meters she would have to break stealth and run to keep up with Markus.

Jack slowly moved across the balcony, clearing the room beyond the French doors as he went. Just across the room opposite to the doors, there was an open closet packed full of clothing hanging on hangers. Jack cleared the bottom of the closet as best he could. Nothing looked suspicious except the blood-soaked drag mark across the carpet leading to a closed bedroom door. Once satisfied, Jack dropped to his knees and placed the pistol back in his chest holster. He then quickly opened the case and took out a Satellite antenna and erected it. The antenna, fully assembled stood about three feet off the ground and connected to the case by a long filament wire. He then attached the antenna to the balcony railing and aligned it to the up and west to capture satellite signals in orbit. He then powered up the case and entered the uplink instructions and access codes. The device began searching for a viable signal for communication which could take several minutes. Just then something caught Jack's eye. He drew his pistol with a flash and scanned the room. The clothes in the closet were swaying back and forth just a little, but the blood covering the glass of the door made it hard to see in the room. Jack wasn't sure if the clothes were swaying before or not. He scanned the bottom of the closet thoroughly but found nothing of interest. Jack blew it off and holstered his weapon. He then turned his attention to the devices search progress.

Lilith was now about 3 meters behind Markus. Keeping up was now becoming a chore and began cursing her short stature when she suddenly bumped into Markus. Instinctively Lilith pushed up against Markus's massive back and index her weapon. She then grabbed the back of his arm with her hand to signal she was ready. His posture was stiff, and his arm tensed and solid. Then she noticed he was shaking. Then came the sound. A sound that sent chills up her spine. Like jagged teeth gnawing on bone and meat. A sickly slow chewing sound. She suddenly felt queasy but suppressed the feeling.

As if Markus was cover, Lilith pulled her weapon in close and began to round Markus's large frame slowly. As she began to crest his side she punched her weapon out... paused... then gasped in horror.

Jack's thoughts wondered for a moment. He was trying to understand what was going on. His feelings were mixed. He was scared, concerned, and bewildered. Sweat dripped from his brow onto the SatCom panel. Nerves were getting to him. As he wiped his forehead with his gloved hand, another feeling swept over him. But this time it wasn't from within his mind.

Scopaesthesia, the sense that someone or something is staring at you. Jack's Scopaesthesia alarms were blowing full bore in his head. His entire body stiffened as he slowly picked up his head and began to scan the room just in front of him. At first, he saw nothing, but he knew something was there and kept looking. After a few moments, he saw it.

Panic and fear shot through his body like hundreds of gallons of cold water was poured over him. His heart started pounding in his chest. He tried to move but couldn't.

There at the bottom of the closet, as if hanging upside down, Jack's stare was locked into a horrid pair of eyes peeking under the lower part of the clothes that hung there. It might have been a little girl once judging from the two small pigtails hanging down. But not anymore. Her skin was gray and streaked with dark blood vessels. Her eyes sunk in her skull unnaturally and they shined black except for her iris's which were white like puss. Blood covered most of her face as if she was finger painting with it and she shivered horribly with an overly excited shocked look on her face.

Paralyzed with fear, Jack tried to call Dave over the radio, but his hand wouldn't move. He tried to call out, but his lungs refused to take a breath.

After a torturously long moment, the creature turned around and slowly crawled down and out of the closet. Naked but not human it made its way to the French doors. The glare and blood covering it obscured Jack's vision, but he knew it was there.   It walked on all fours like an ape knuckling the floor, but it moved catlike. Its gaze never leaving Jacks. It crept slowly to the window like a mischievous feline teasing its prey. It stopped at the door and impishly peered out. Jacks could see it's horrid face clearer now. Its nose was no more the two slits in its face, and its mouth was packed full of jagged teeth attached to black gums that spanned the entire width of its head. It dropped its head slightly and smiled. Jack could hardly fathom the number of teeth it had.

Still locked in a gaze with Jack the creature slowly reached up and grabbed the doorknob. It began to salivate uncontrollably as it slowly turned the knob. Jack heard an audible click as the door unlatched and it opened it slowly with a creek.

There in a clearing, thirty meters in front of Markus and Lilith, stood a grotesque figure. It stood about fourteen feet and may have weighed a thousand pound. It looked as if a fat man did too many steroids and grew up to this thing. Pale and almost hairless with arms that could reach the ground as it stood upright. Its legs seem shorter than normal for a creature its height, but everything about it wasn't normal. It had its back turned to them and appeared to be chewing on something.

Just then Lilith saw movement behind the bulbous creature and turned her attention to it. To her horror, she saw a young woman dazed and terrified. She was covered in blood and debris and barely able to hold her head up. Both her legs and one arm appeared to have been gnawed off, and the stumps crudely tied off with a tourniquet that looked entirely too tight. She was trying to crawl away with her one good arm, but creature would pull her back to its side by a bloody rope. Each time she would sob in frustration and then in a moment try again. It became horrifyingly apparent that this thing was eating one of her limbs while she was alive… and watching.

Ten feet separated Jack and the thing from the closet. He was still unable to move, and although he was screaming inside and flailing about like a crazy junky, he couldn't get his body to move. All he could do was grunt now and then.

"*PLEASE GOD LET ME MOVE!! LET ME GET MY FUCKING GUN!!! IT'S RIGHT THERE INCHES FROM MY HAND!! GIVE ME MY BODY BACK YOU FUCKING GOUL!*' Jack screamed in his head.

The creature crouched down and prepared to pounce on its prey like a cat. It's gaping mouth drooling in anticipation of the fresh Jack flesh. As Jack watched, paralyzed with fear, panic began to boil up in his mind. He struggled but could only force out a faint quivering groan.

Just then the computer connected to the satellite and the computer beeped that it had completed its task.

As if the beep was a starter pistol, both Jack and the creature initiated their assault on each other with blinding speed. Jack, shocked back to life by the sudden noise, drew his pistol with blinding speed as the creature came flying at him with incredible quickness. Jack unloaded ten .45 caliber Hydro Shock rounds into the creature as he rolled backward and sent the thing flying over the balcony and into the back yard as it screamed bloody horror!

Dave jerked back a step from the sudden and unannounced gunfire. He immediately began a cold sweat from head to toe.

Then, in bewilderment, Dave saw the creature launch from the balcony and onto the ground just behind a shrub twenty meters away screaming an awful scream the entire way. Dave couldn't quite tell what the thing was he saw, but once it hit the ground, it began to flail about kicking up dirt and debris in a blinding rage. After a moment, it stopped.

Dave took a couple of steps forward to get a closer look. Still shocked from the sudden noise and confused as to what he just saw he just stood there scanning. As the dust finally settled, Dave suddenly wished he was up on the balcony with Jack.

There just behind the shrub was the creature from the closet standing on its hind legs and panting heavily. Then it saw Dave and froze.

Dave squinted trying to see the thing clearly when he realized it was looking right at him. Dave's eye widened in surprise at the horror of the creature and took an uneasy step back.

Then, without warning, it pulled in a deep breath, let out a horrid scream, then charged Dave with blinding speed. Dirt and debris shot everywhere as the powerful creature's claws scampered through the brush and across the lawn.

"HOLY FUCK!" Dave gasped

Jack's gunshots spooked the massive creature. It grunted and stood upright with a jerk looking around for the cause of the sound. Wobbling under its own weight, it turned around slowly. Both Lilith and Markus could see its face clearly now. Lilith immediately placed her hand over her mouth in disgust.

It's head and shoulders almost appeared as one.

The skin on its skull hung thin and loose on its head. It had no other features other than two small holes where its eyes should have been. Its mouth was of average width, but it opened almost half way down its sternum and bared teeth that resembled horse teeth. Blood and gore stained its fat belly. It looked around quickly as its jowls jiggled back and forth till it finally saw Markus and little Lilith behind him.

Surprised the two were there the creature gasping and took a step back. It was at that moment Lilith couldn't take it anymore. She kept watching the girl on the rope and knew she was suffering horribly. The girl was looking back at Lilith and almost lethargically begged Lilith to kill her.

Lilith didn't hesitate and stepped to the side taking careful aim. In only a moment acquired her sights and fired one round. The bullet hit the girl in the head just about her eye killing her instantly.

The creature, shocked, jumped back and looked at the girl confused. It the tugged on the rope and whimpered a little. In its other hand, it had the girls leg. Then, like a child throwing a tantrum, it grunted loudly and threw the leg to the side in protest.   Lilith, now fully exposed to the creature sights lifted up her none firing hand, flipped off the creature and yelled...

"YEAH WELL FUCK YOU FAT ASS!"

The creature became enraged tossing the rope to the side and roared loudly while flexing its overdeveloped flabby arms.

"Kill it!" Lilith ordered Markus, who was all too willing to cooperate.

Leveling their weapons both began pumping round after round into the bloated creature as it held up its arms defensively. But soon their guns needed reloading, and that gave the creature time to retaliate.

It dropped its arms to its side and shook its hands as if they were numb. Then it looked up, roared and sprang forward on all fours like an angry ape.

"FUCK... RUN!" Markus yelled. Sprinting away, the two finished their reload on the fly and heading straight towards the road.

Shrieking loudly, the wounded friend from the closet advanced on Dave with increasable speed and ferocity. Dave fumbled with his M14 rifle as if he had never held one before and was able to get off one good round impacting into the forehead of the once little girl.

Its head exploded feet from where Dave was standing covering him with razor sharp teeth, bone and brain matter. A moment later the headless body impacted Dave's chest like a wet sack of cement knocking him to the ground. Jack reached the railing with his SCAR at the ready. There he saw Dave on his back in a pool of gore. He had a shocked look on his face as he spit gristle and bone from his mouth.

"I'm coming down!" Jack stated in a panic.

"What... the... fuck..." Dave replied in a squeaky voice thoroughly disgusted.

In the distance, the two could hear rapid gunfire and assumed Markus and Lilith were involved. Setting aside their inner astonishment as to what just took place they both sprinted to the front of the house. Joe and the others soon arrived from within the house.

"Dave, Jack! Report!" Joe ordered.

"It was scary!" Dave replied almost too quickly. Jack stood at his side nodding in agreement. The two just stood there with wide eyes as if they just got caught by their mother with a porno mag.

Joe noticed that Dave was covered head to toe in blood and gore.

"I'm only assuming it's dead right?" Joe asked

"Uh... Sure..." Dave replied spitting what he believed was the little girl's hair from his mouth.

Markus and Lilith came busting out of the wood line in a dead sprint about one hundred meters up the road firing widely behind them. Once they hit the road, they split up on both sides and ran to the house as fast as they could yelling "INCOMING!"

Just then the group could hear a quiet but astonishingly powerful thrumping sound. It got louder and louder every time they heard it till suddenly the globular mass of a creature exploded out of the woods roaring wildly. It's bulbous body covered in the blood of its victims and now also its own. Zeroing in on Lilith it began its charge down the street after her.

Everyone took a step back, and a let out a simultaneous "WWHHOOAA!" and stood there unable to process the scene in front of them.

Lilith, sensing something was wrong, fired her pistol in the direction of the house slamming her .45 round into the side on one of the trucks thus waking up the guys and getting them moving again.

The entire crew leveled off their weapons and began firing into the portly creatures disgusting body. Lilith and Markus didn't slow down, but they did make sure they were running in a straight line as hundreds of rounds blasted by them by only a few feet. The air around them whizzed and spat as munitions of all sizes shrieked by them.

The creature didn't slow at first, but the onslaught took its toll on it, and it finally succumbed and stopped raising its arm defensively.

Joe then took out a grenade and pulled the pin with a jerk.

"Frag out!" he yelled and chucked it as hard as he could. Both Lilith and Markus hit the ground on either side of the road. The grenade hit the ground within five meters of the beast and exploded shredding the right side of the creature. Reeling in pain, it let out a horrid scream and began batting at the air as if it could swat the pain away.

"Markus! Throw a grenade!" Lilith yelled.

Markus was already a step ahead, but they were close. He pulled the pin, let the spoon fly and cooked off three seconds on the five-second fuse. Markus then tossed the grenade at the feet of the creature hoping to cause the most damage. Within moments the grenade exploded blasting a significant portion of the creature in every direction. Gore and filth filled the air as Lilith and Markus jumped to their feet and sprinted away.

"COVER!" Joe yelled as everyone scattered. Lilith and Markus made it under the trucks just in time as chunks of gore and lard began landing around them. The larger chunks impacted hit the ground spattering blood and bits of entrails all over the crew. Most of the crew didn't have time to get to cover. The entire situation happened so fast. Moments later the gruesome storm ceased its hellish salvo.

The crew held their positions for a moment just listening ensuring everything had calmed down before moving around. Discipline told them to stay quiet and just observe their surroundings. However, the stench of the gore about them was enough to make even the strongest man gag. Discipline in the group broke down quickly. Grunts and groans manifested in the quiet and then several members began cursing aloud with no regards to security.

Dave, now covered in the internals of two creatures was holding his own quite well. Wide eyed he turned to Jack and asked him politely if he would be so kind as to hose him off. Jack, just as wide-eyed, nodded and the two walked off without a word.

Lilith rolled out from under the truck. Although she was breathing heavy, she was not scared at all. The others, however, were in a bit of a daze trying to mentally digest what just happened in the last twenty-four hours. Not Lilith though. To her, this almost seemed familiar.

Without an escort, she slowly walked down the road to the now Disembowel creature. Its body jerked and quivered as it laid in the ditch on the side of the road. Most of its lower half spread over a twenty-meter area, but it may still be alive she thought. As she rounded to the back side of the ditch, she could see its face. It was astonished and quickly turned to her with rage gurgling a silent scream as it tried to reach for her. Lilith didn't react.

Then something happened that disturbed her immensely. The creature seemed to have recognized her. It stopped reaching for her suddenly and had a look on its grotesque face as if it had figured out something.

Then it seemed to cower. Almost groveling.

In the distance, Lilith heard Joe call for her as he approached but she ignored him. Then she remembered the young girl in the woods and how she must have suffered.

Rage filled her lungs like thick hot smoke. With blinding speed, she drew her pistol from her chest rig and slammed two rounds into the creature's head.

What was left of its revolting carcass sunk heavy in the grass as air gurgled from its mouth.

"Jesus! Was that thing still alive!" Joe asked as he ran up beside her.

"Barly, but yeah it was."

Joe stroked his beard completely perplexed as to what just happened. He often stroked his beard when dealing with a decision or just in deep thought. Lilith, however, seemed almost aggravated more than anything.

"Let's get back to cover Crazy Ass."

Lilith turned to Joe and looked him straight in the eyes. He met her gaze and looked deep into hers. He could see she was sad. Not sad like she lost a friend but sad as in deep in her soul. He placed his heavily tattooed arm around her waist and pulled her in close. She buried her face in his chest as he held her tight. Although the stench from the creature was thick in the air, the only thing she could smell was Joe's beard oil. Cedar and spice. Lilith imagined that he smelled like a pirate. Just at that moment, she felt normal. But that feeling quickly dissipated.

"Joe... please don't ever change." Lilith pleaded holding back tears.

"Never." Joe replied with conviction.

Everyone was able to take a shower at the side of the house with the garden hose. Nobody ever went back in the house. The house seemed to grow creepier by the minute, and it made keeping good security almost impossible. At least that was their excuse anyway.

They changed clothes and discarded their soiled clothing in the woods. Even if they were able to to do laundry, nobody wanted their old clothes after what happened.

Joe stood guard for Lilith with his back to her. She washed up by herself while the others prepared the trucks for movement.

After a few attempts, Jack was able to get in contact with a Colonel Montgomery in Kentucky. He and a significant amount of mixed Armed Forces are held up in the Waverly Hills Sanatorium, Louisville, Kentucky holding a line of resistance against the hellish Army invaders. They were only a few hundred miles away. It was far but not an impossible trip.

Over the next twenty minutes, Joe spoke to the group. He had no idea what was going on, but he knew that they had to deal with the situation no matter how fantastic it was.

"Obviously I'm not going to give you the old "there's a perfectly good explanation for this" talk. But, it appears an event has occurred, and it doesn't change who we are." Joe sighed and stroked his beard, thinking.

"Jack..." Joe said.

"Yes Joe." Jack answered stepping forward. His tone was humble, but he knew what was about to come.

"They captured one."

"I understand." Jack replied humbly. Joe told the Colonel that Jack is an accomplished interrogator and that he would conduct the interrogation of the prisoner as soon as they arrived. Interrogations can go one of two ways. Jack can break down the subject mentally… or physically. Although his techniques are potently effective, the latter can be soul consuming for both men. Jack is a good person, but he has done some horrifying things to people during his life in the name of freedom. Some of which changed him forever.   Jack stepped up and explained the rest of the mission and provided a simple security brief.

"We are going to link up with a supply convoy about thirty miles from here and assimilate into their security. One of the trucks broke down. Only two personnel for security and the two drivers are it. We can get ammo and medical from them. Dave has the rally point, so he's in the lead. As for some good news! Val and Monty secured a plane in Arizona and are on their way here! Or well… to the Sanitarium at least."

Everyone let out a very hushed cheer. That was good news and knowing their friends were safe substantially raised their morale.

"Thanks Jack. Mount up." Joe ordered.

CHAPTER 7
"Convoy to the Sanitarium"

It didn't take long to find the downed freight truck on the side of the road. Although Joe called in their approach, the security team was nowhere to be found.

"What do you mean they just walked off?" Joe asked the pudgy truck driver.

"They said they were going to set up a 'Security Over There' or something." The trucker stated in a thick country accent than spit dip on the ground.

"You mean a 'Security Over Watch'?" Joe replied.

"Sure whatever. I've learned to do what they say and don't argue. They got my shit out of some pretty tight hoopla the last couple of days."

Dave walked up and tapped Joe on the arm and motioned down the road. It was dusk, but they both could see two individuals walking up. One a male and one a female. Both in their thirties and dressed in black business wear with white dress shirts and black ties making them look very "Men in Black." With dirt, blood, and torn seams randomly about their attire confirmed they had been consistently fighting for several days. The female, however, had on a black skirt that seemed to have ripped up the side exposing an extremely muscular thigh. Her hair was pulled back in a ponytail and looked as if it had been through a lot. The male had short light brown hair, almost blond and displayed notable two-day growth on his face.

Joe wasn't sure what drew his attention more. Was it that fact that their fitted black suits covered what appeared to be an extremely fit couple or was it that fact that they also wore thick black framed coke bottle glasses making them very odd characters.

As they approached Joe noticed they both had matching Herra Arms AR15 style rifles with a blue, green and red shatter pattern Cerakote painted on them, effectively break up the rifles silhouette. Joe, impressed as to how effective it was, made a mental note to get his like that if they ever get out of this situation.

"The fuck are these guys?" Dave whispered under his breath.

"I don't know, but those guns are no joke." Joe replied.

Dave then chuckled.

"You ever see the movie 'Six String Samurai'?" Dave asked comparing the odd couple to the main character Buddy.

"That's one of my favorites Bro!" Joe stated as the two fist pounded their bromance moment.

The peculiar couple approached, and Joe could finally see their faces up close. They both adorned very similar features. Both had strongly defined jaw lines and dark blue eyes. Although the female was a beautiful woman, she wore no makeup and almost appeared awkward and very tomboyish in her stance.

Just then Lilith walked up and stood beside Joe.

"Looks like you finally have someone to play with." Joe stated under his breath.

"Good to see I'm not the only one having a bad hair day." Lilith stated nonchalantly referring to the woman walking up.

When the two approached, the woman spoke first.

"My name is Isabella Njoror. This is Danny, my brother. You must be Joe no?" the female asked in a thick Icelandic accent.

"Yes, this is Dave, my Bravo team leader, and this is Lilith, our advisor. We have two up-armored SUV's and ten men available." Joe stated. Dave elbowed Joe in the arm gently. He was trying to remind him inconspicuously of Wess.

"I'm sorry... we have nine men available. We will take the lead and trail accordingly. Command said we could get a resupply as well."

The two glanced at each other. They knew Joe had lost a guy at some point, but they were impressed that they only lost one person. Most groups they meet up with are at least twenty percent strength.

"I'm sorry for your loss. Please excuse my manner. We have little time. Ammo and Guns are in here. Med, food, armor in there." Danny pointed to the freight rigs and then turned to the driver.

"Just like we said, ok guys? I assume you fixed the battery?"

"Yeah boss. We's good here." The two truck drivers replied and ran off to their respective vehicles.

Isabella walked up to Dave and pulled out a small thumb drive like device with a with wire attached to a small plastic tag. On the tag read the numbers 1204.

"Here are the net keys for your ANCD. Don't lose that key it is the only one we got left ok? We will move out in blackout.

Do let everyone know to NOD up. Also, if we take contact, we push through. We don't have time for battle drills you know." Isabella said handing Dave the key.

"Got it. Thanks." Dave ran off and started working on the comms key encryption. Once complete he took his team up to the front and re-checked comms again. In ten minutes they were on the road.

"Ok. Keep along this road for about 20 miles. We will be making a right onto a dirt road. It's level but dusty so be aware Trail Vehicle. Break." Danny paused for a second. Everyone patiently waited knowing the break in the transmission was to keep the enemy from triangulating their position.

"About 15 miles from the site we will secure the vehicles in the woods and use Helios the rest of the way. It's safest that way, but it's going to be a fight ok? Over." Danny finished

Dave and Joe came over the radio one at a time and confirmed they understood the message.

It was dark now, and there was a new moon out. Everyone had NVG's at the ready or mounted to their weapons. Isabella gave directions from the freight truck as the convoy cruised slowly down the road.

Then suddenly out of nowhere, Isabella came over the radio.

"Stop here! Lead and trail dismount and set up security up and down the road. No lights, no noise!"

Everyone did as they were told. Danny climbed up on top of his freight truck and watched as Joe's team moved out. He was impressed and had a good idea why they lasted so long. Dome lights were deactivated so when they exited their vehicles they wouldn't announce their location. Joe's team set security in seconds and was ready for anything. Everyone gave thumbs up once security was set. Danny never even heard them.

Danny turned and saw his sister on the lead freight truck roof overseeing the security setup in front. Once the lead security was set, she turned to Danny and gave him a thumbs up.

"Quick brief." Isabella's voice came over the radio after a few moments.

"Spector gunship reports two hundred plus troops in the open... about our ten o'clock two hundred meters out moving parallel to our position possibly heading... never mind..." Isabella suddenly signed off without an explanation. Joe was about to break the silence when the Spector began unloading various ordinance on the two hundred or so troops.

Like a dragon in the sky flames and tracers of all types appeared out of nowhere and started slamming into the ground. Thunder erupted as the artillery rounds exploded rumbling through the ground beneath them as if they were laying on Jello. Red light crept through between the trees eerily. Screams and random gunfire could be heard in the distance but were overwhelmed by the Spector's assault.

"I don't care how many times this happens… Those Spectators gunships are fucking impressive." Markus whispered to Jack.

Jack, also impressed, didn't say anything but the look in his eyes was enough for Markus. With a smile on his face, he mouthed the words "Holy Shit" silently.

Then, without warning, Lilith jumped up and sprinted to the lead truck.

"What the fuck is she doing Damnit! She'll give us away!" Isabella yelled over the radio. Joe responded, but it was not what Isabella wanted to hear.

"READY UP!" Joe shouted aloud breaking the noise discipline.

Everyone cursed under their breath as Lilith bolted.

Reaching the lead truck, she jumped onto the hood effortlessly and took up aim in almost the complete opposite direction as the Spector conflict.

"Is she insane. There's nothing there!" Isabella protested again over the radio.

Lilith clicked off safe to full auto and began firing into the sky as four low-flying Messerschmitt BF 190 Fighter planes flew just overhead screaming at full throttle. Smoke and exhaust poured from their engine compartments as they flew over. One Messerschmitt burst into flames as Lilith managed to find its fuel tanks.

"Again! One o'clock! Ready!" Lilith yelled aiming her weapon to the one o'clock. Rear security held their positions, but everyone else set up in the middle of the road and targeted where Lilith was marking.

Lilith quickly did a magazine exchange and loaded a magazine full of just tracer round.

"Shoot here!" she yelled and began firing tracers just down the road and over the trees. Everyone else followed suit as four more BF 190's blasted by at the same time. This time they were able to take out two aircraft.

Lilith stopped firing and turned to Isabella.

"Call in air support or that Spector is dead! We have to go! Mount up!" Lilith yelled.

Isabella, a little shocked at what she just saw tried to call in support. Her efforts, however, were short-lived when the three A-10 Thunderbolts soared by in pursuit of the Messerschmitt fighters. Thier 30mm Avenger cannons blasting away. Fire and hot brass exploded everywhere as everyone hit the ground for cover.

Isabella rolled off the top of the rig and landed on the ground facing Lilith who was already back on her feet and heading to the trucks.

"Pretty fast with that air support!" Lilith stated somewhat sarcastically.

Isabella didn't know what to say. She was stunned. Lilith and her team just shot down three aircraft Isabella didn't even know were there. She quickly got to her feet and turned to see her brother coming up fast.

"I'm good! Let's get out of here!" she yelled. Time was not on their side. Danny held his hands up and then turned and ran to his freight truck. Their position was now exposed, and they still had ten miles to move.

"Give me a check when your teams are up?" Isabella commanded over the radio.
Each team checked in, and Isabella gave the order to move out straight ten miles.

Lilith checked her weapon and reloaded another mag without tracers. She then popped the out the sunroof with Markus. There wasn't a lot of room, but Lilith wiggled her little body in even at Markus's protest. She didn't want to miss the Dogfight. Lilith knew it was going to be amazing. After a few moments, she decided it was everything she thought it was going to be. Amazing.

Through the NOD's she could see that the Spector had taken some damage. Not risking further damage it hightailed it back to wherever it was from, low and fast and dumping flares as it went.

The A10's were not designed for Air to Air battles but seem to be holding their own in the sky. The whole thing was over in a matter of minutes.

"Yes!" Lilith shouted fist pumping the air.

"Ok! Ok! You fucking weirdo. Get in the truck. They kill the bad guys." Markus said pushing Lilith down by the top of her head.

"Alright! I'm moving!"

After what seemed like forever the convoy arrived at their location. It was a small farm just off the road. Isabella had Joe and his crew pull the trucks into the farmhouse garage and told them to grab whatever they could that might be useful while she and her brother pulled the rigs into the field.

Within moments they had unhitched the Cabs, and the drivers moved them into a barn not far away. Danny and Isabella stayed with the Freight cars for security.

"Joe get your guys to pull security 360 for a helo pick up. It's going to be quick. First two helos get the rigs. The next two for the drivers and half the security and then two more for the rest of us. Got it?" Danny stated over the radio. He directed the call to Joe, but everyone heard and moved to their perspective areas of responsibility.

Joe's team set up a cordon a hundred meters and 360 degrees around the freighters to include a sniper/observer team over watch nearby. The action took mere moments and was coordinated without a sound.

Danny called up a sitrep on the teams to ensure accountability and forwarded the info to the helos en route

"Two minutes. As I said, this will go fast so keep your head down and do not hesitate, or you'll get left behind." Danny called out again.

Dave and Jack were in the trees conducting overwatch. Both men peered through high-powered

NVGs trying to find anything they could call a target. Jack noticed movement on the far side of the perimeter but couldn't make it out.

"Farside element this is overwatch. You have movement to your two o'clock. Right side shed. Looks like shadows from here. Over." Jack called over the radio. Dave immediately moved his rifle to where Jack called and took over observations. Jack then moved to scanning the perimeter again.

"On it!"

"What did you see Jack?" Dave whispered.

"Not sure. It looked like someone was peeking around the corner of the woodshed by the wood line but it happened too quick. Maybe nothing." Jack responded. They both knew it was something as the hairs on the backs of their necks stood on end.

Mike and Mitch adjusted their position to face the shed and examined the shed from top to bottom.

"Nothing. Shed door is locked." Mike called out over the radio.

"One minute. We need that shed cleared. I have you covered." Danny replied raising his weapon up.

"Roger, Moving." Mike stated and tapped Mitch on the shoulder. The two popped up and moved adjacent to the shed to clear the backside. Each man quick and steady with weapons at the ready. As Mike began to breach around the sheds corner, he slowed down, and Mitch took a knee. Mike slowly moved around the corner until he could see the backside of the shed. There, he saw something.

"Got something." Mike stated.

"Clarify!" Danny demanded.

"Something could be anything in this day of age!"

Even though he had Night Vision sights, the image was only a silhouette. He pulled the sights down, blinded and raised his weapon back up. Still no change.

"It's a person. Unknown. Just standing there." Mike reported. Helicopters could be heard in the distance. They were out of time.

"Kill it!" Danny ordered.

"What the Fuck Bro?!?" Mike returned.

Mike didn't know what to do and took up aim. He didn't have a positive identification and knew it was too dangerous to just start killing things. But the image has changed.

"... what the..." Mike spoke aloud.

The silhouette appeared human in a way until it somehow bent over backward in a manner that would have killed the average man. Then spun around on all fours kicking up dust like a creepy spider.

"Damn it! Kill it!" Danny called out aloud.

"Mike what is it!" Mitch yelled.

"I don't know... It's... wait!" Mike yelled back.

The helicopter was just a few hundred meters out and could be seen moving in fast but cautiously, ready to bail on the mission at the first sign of trouble. Discipline held Mikes course tight. Mike knew that he had no business pulling the trigger until he knew precisely what he was killing. And he still wasn't sure yet.

Danny and Isabella both pulled out flairs and prepared to wave off the helicopters. They couldn't afford to lose any aircraft right now, and this could be the end of any future combat missions for the command if the supply freighters don't get to the asylum safe.

Suddenly the figure moved again, and Mike blazed it with the IR light on his rifle. All he could see was teeth and four eyes reflecting back at him.

"FUCK! Good enough!" he yelled and opened fire. Mitch followed suit slamming first a forty millimeter grenade and then three round bursts. Danny and Isabella joined in, and the rest of the group held fast.

The shed went first and exploded as soon as the grenade hit throwing the silhouette into the woodline. Then tracers and .50 caliber rounds started in from the helicopters door gunners. Beastly screams could be heard erupting from the smoke and fire of the woodline. Now and then a clawed leg or a disfigured head emerged just long enough to make you wonder what the fuck you just saw. Two Chinook helicopter banked hard to a stop with their nose in the sky just over the freight cars, and two Blackhawk helicopters pulled around them quickly and began circling the perimeter as low and as fast as they could with their door gunners blasting away with their miniguns.

Suddenly, door gunners from the Blackhawks started calling out targets for the ground crew.

"Movement front!"
"Three targets in the open two o'clock!" Joe finally
came over the radio with his deep voice.

"Open suppression! Overwatch move out!"
everyone with a gun began firing in all directions. Then
suddenly Hellfires from two Cobra's gunships blasted
overhead killing something big behind the farmhouse.

"Watch out Gunships we got trucks in there!"
Joe shouted over the radio.

"Roger!" Someone returned. Joe only assumed
it was the pilot of the Cobras.

Danny and Isabella got the freight trailers
hooked up in seconds, and the two Monstrous
Helicopters powered up slamming everything under
them into a hurricane force winds. Danny and Isabella
didn't even get off the Freight trailers and rode them
off into the distance.

Then without pause two Blackhawks swooped
in and landed with incredible speed and agility. The
gunners continued to fire suppression over and by
everyone moving for extraction.

"Bravo and overwatch move up and take off."
Joe yelled over the radio. The Cobras darted over again
hammering more of the woodline with hellfire missiles
and twenty-millimeter rounds. Dave and Jack sprinted
from the same wood line and darted across the road.
Not far behind and closing quick were two dog-like
creatures the size of bears. Fangs and Teeth snapped
violently in anticipation of fresh flesh.

"Shit! Cover Overwatch!" Joe yelled firing at
the doglike creatures. The Cobras saw the pursuit and

pulled a quick turn taking up aim on the creatures. Letting loose with their cannons they were able to hit the creatures. One hit the ground as if it fell out of the sky rolling to a stop. The other one, however, leaped at Jack. Jack tucked and rolled as soon as he felt the creature at his back. Dave turned and fired relentlessly into the beast's side and head. The Cobras darted overhead engaging other targets just to the other end of the perimeter.

Dave ran over to Jack yelling his name. Jack was on his back trying to get up. He was stunned but seemed ok.

"Holy fuck! Get up Jack this is no place to be on your back!" Dave yelled as he reloaded.

Once Jack was up the two bolted to the helicopters and jumped in with Bravo team. Dave gave the Crew Chief the thumbs up letting him know they were good. Everyone then took up positions to the left and right of the minigunners and began laying suppressive fire out the gunner's door at anything moving. Nothing was getting in the perimeter.

The Crew Chief gave the pilot the thumbs up, and the two Blackhawks pulled away quickly replaced with by two more Blackhawks.

Suddenly artillery rounds started coming in blasting dirt and shrapnel in all directions.

"Alpha team move! Incoming!" Joe yelled over the radio as everyone made a mad dash for the helicopters cursing as they went. Bravo team circled overhead in the Blackhawks providing Alpha team much-needed cover fire. Once Alpha team boarded

Blackhawk, Joe took a quick personnel inventory and gave the crew chief a thumbs up. In less than a few moments, they all shot out of the area as artillery rounds destroyed the landing zone.

Lilith sat back in her seat of the Blackhawk shaking off some of the dizziness. Things went from quiet to a feeding frenzy in less than a few seconds. She would never admit it aloud, but she lived for moments like this. Trying hard to hold back her enthusiasm she let out a sly grin. Joe and Markus noticed and shook their heads in amusement.

"Don't relax just yet. We have to fly over part of the front line. All guns to the doors!" The Crew Chief yelled out.

Everyone moved to the doors and began scanning their sector when out of nowhere twenty-millimeter rounds blasted by the Blackhawks from behind closely followed by two A10 Thunderbolts with their Avenger guns blazing. The concussion blast and heat from the A10's weapons system hit the team like a slap in the face.

Everyone was shocked at how close the Thunderbolt was. Apparently, safety is less of a concern.

Just as the A10's past by, the door gunners swung out and began blazing away with their miniguns. Both teams moved to the doors and provide fire support as best as they could. Enemy tracer fire and anti-aircraft Flak filled the air around them but hurled off into the distance unable to find their target. The Blackhawk pilots were flying Nap of the Earth, banking hard left and right only feet off the tree line making them impossible marks.

"FUCK YEAHHHHHH!" Lilith yelled over the radio completely unable to contain her enthusiasm anymore as she unloaded magazine after magazine on various targets. Both Alpha and Bravo teams joined in the festivity yelling and cursing the enemy as they mowed down a path to the asylum.

Tanks, trooper, and field artillery filled the landscape of the now burned out forest. The invading army illuminated by burning trees and muzzle flashes. The A10's and the helicopter convoy not far behind cut a huge rift in the line destroying everything in their path. It was incredibly one-sided.

After a few moments, the Crew Chief yelled a cease-fire as everyone reluctantly pulled in their weapons. With big smiles on their faces, the teams called in their status. Lilith and Markus high-fived each other as the Blackhawks pulled a hard bank and then landed.

"Time to go! Bad Ass work Fucker!!" the Crew Chief yelled and pointed to the wood line. Lilith turned and saw a four hummer convoy giving over watch for the helicopters on the landing pad. Monty and Val accompanied the convoy still wearing their bright orange jumpsuits. The team unbuckled, grabbed their packs, and sprinted across the field to the trucks. Joe, counting his troops on the way, was soon met by the Convoy Commander who was accompanied by an older gentleman.

"I'm Colonel Montgomery! Are you Joe?!" The

older man yelled. The Colonel, still wearing an oversized Realtree jacket and Realtree overalls from a hunting trip cut short, shook Joe's hand firmly. No salutes here.

"Yes Sir…" Joe stated not realizing he sounded stunned.

"Ah Yeah… Um.. I was hunting. I haven't even had a chance to change." He replied at the obvious concern in Joe's voice. The two paused as the last two helicopters flew off.

The group spent a minute giving Monty and Val some Bro Hugs. Then it was Lilith's turn. She scolded them at first for getting in trouble but was soon hugging them as if they were brothers long missed. Suddenly it was eerily quiet. The Colonel looked at Joe with concerned eyes.

"I'm going to brief you when we get in. I need your full attention Joe. We have a shit storm here." The colonel stated in a calm voice. He spoke softly, but it sounded loud and piercing in the now quiet night hair. The whole team looked at each other nervously.

Joe and the team made it to the Asylum. It was an old building that stood almost five stories high and made of reinforced concrete and steel beams. In its time, Joe imagined it was probably an impressive building. But today it's rather decrepit state of ruin made it look like a perfect place for a horror movie. Not a light could be seen. It was to keep them safe from enemy artillery, but it made the building look even grimmer and eerily spooky.

CHAPTER 8
"Going Deep"

Joe and the team eat a quick meal of T-Rations and Oranges. Nothing new to them anyway. Once finished the team loaded up on ammo and medical supplies. They were in decent spirits laughing and joking with each other. Joe observed them closely looking for anything that might be out of the ordinary with his men. He cared only for his team, more than himself and tried very hard to keep them sound. They seemed good considering what they just went through.

Lilith was looking at Joe. He took care of the team, and she took care of him. She knew Joe was upset that Wess didn't make it, but she knew it wasn't Joe's fault. She just hoped he was aware of that as well. The look on his face didn't make her think so.

Lilith grabbed her rifle and walked over to where Joe stood. She then stood on the chair next to him so that she was a little taller than him. Looking over Joe smiled.

"I'm fine Lilith." He said as he turned back to his team.

"You're kidding, right?! You are the sickest fucker in here." She said teasing him. Joe shot her a look. It was a look that said he was about to say something sarcastic. It was just what she was looking for. Joe was good. At least for now. But before Joe was able to speak Danny walked in.

"Jack your up. Get you team and come with me." Danny said loud enough for everyone to hear.

Jack walked by Joe and Lilith; he looked nervous. It wasn't like he lacked talent in finding information. Jack was a pro at digging things out of people that don't want to talk. The only problem Jack had no idea what he was confronting and where it came from. Did it have a soul? Could it bleed? Jack shrugged it off and decided that those were the first two things he was going to find out. The thing is really in control. It determines how far they both go down the rabbit hole. He was willing to go all the way. It's not like he hasn't before. Even though he may lose some of his soul in the process, things were bad. Time to man up and sacrifice.

But that was Jack. In his mind, he could recover. At least he hoped he could. Most people would implode and self-decimate themselves. But not Jack. He was a rock. It was incredible how he could just let it go. At least he gave that appearance.

As Jack walked by Lilith grabbed him by the arm and looked deep into his eyes. Jack stopped and looked back at her. He let the connection sit for a second but time is of the essence.

"I will do what is needed Lilith. You know this. It is for the better good." Jack stated.

"Jack... I could care less about what you do to the poor bastard. Torture him all day for all I care. I just worry about you." Lilith exclaimed.

"We have work to do. Maybe I'll get lucky, and he'll know who I am and tell us everything." Jack returned somewhat joking.

Lilith let go of his arm, and he turned and walked towards the door. There Danny stopped him and turned to the rest of the group.

"The Colonel wants everyone. You've gotta see this." Danny stated to Jack's surprise. The whole team glanced at each other and slowly got up. Everyone was a little surprised and not sure they wanted to see Jack's magic interviews. Markus once overheard Jack at work and wished he never did. Reluctantly, they followed.

They soon arrived at two doors at the end of a long hallway deep in the basement of the asylum. The hallway smelled old and damp like a creepy basement should smell. The halogen lights smeared a sick light on the paint peeled walls giving the everyone an uncomfortable apprehensive feeling. The presence of the ten Army Soldiers in full combat gear didn't help ease the feeling either.

"Jack, Joe… you come with me. Everyone else, go into the observation room there ok?" Danny directed, but Joe interrupted.

"Lilith will go with us." Joe insisted. Danny didn't care either way and nodded in agreement.

"No guns ok?"

Jack had already handed off his side arm, and Joe had only his M4 which he gave to Markus. Lilith, however, was having trouble with her belt. The rig was attached to an inner belt. It was a very secure and comfortable set up but a pain to get on and off.

"Go in... I'll catch up." She told Joe. The three men then turned and walked in the room.

The room was octagon shaped and appeared bigger than expected. The floor and walls composed of Concrete with two sets of hanging halogen lights. It looked like this room was designed for medical procedures where other doctors could watch from overhead in the observation chambers. The rest of the team entered the observation room and sat down. A long table with various medical instruments sat against the wall nearest the door. The only other thing in the room was a steel bar cage about twenty feet by twenty feet and in that cage, pacing frantically was a heavily muscled man only clothed in old German Infantry pants.

His skin, hairless, was bleached white and waxy in appearance. Nowhere on his body could an ounce of fat be found. Deep scars and dark vessels peppered his body making him look almost dead. When the team walked in the thing seemed to ignore them as if they were not even there. It paced away vigorously breathing aloud like a caged animal.

Jack suddenly felt his heart stop. This Man... thing. It was not going to break easily, if at all. He cursed in his head. But he was there. Maybe this thing was putting up a front. Maybe it was scared already Jack thought. Joe and Danny stopped just shy of the Cage while Jack walked up to it ensuring he was at least arm's length away. The man reached the other end of the cage and turned around with purpose. He saw Jack and zeroed in on him. Jack tried to speak, but his thoughts caught him off guard. This man's eyes were a brilliant ice blue. A blue that practically glowed with an almost psycho awareness of Jacks thoughts. Chills ran up his back. Then there was the man's lower jaw which appeared to have been made crudely of iron with a wire mess where his teeth should have been. The creature moved quick and lunged at Jack slamming its body into the bars with enough force to kill an ordinary man. It reached out for Jacks' neck with blood stained hands. They lingered there just centimeters away from Jacks' face. Jack, who already felt anxious, tried not to react at all. Joe and Danny, however, took a step back and quickly assumed a fight stance. After a few moments, Jack took a breath and prepared to say something. The two were locked eye to eye as the creature desperately tried to grab Jack. Nothing but rage filled its face. This thing wanted Jack dead, and he wanted him dead badly. Jack focused. He was all in and knew this was going to be messy. He figured he would go through the introductions and then ask the team to leave. Nobody needed to see this but Jack and the creature. *Those eyes though!*

The door clicked as Lilith closed it behind her. She slowly moved behind Danny and Joe trying not to draw attentions to herself. The creature glanced at the new noise and paused. Its demeanor changed instantly from a savage beast to nervous child. Jack noticed it almost appeared worried or something. It scanned desperately to see Lilith from behind the two large men and moved frantically to the cage bars nearest her for a better look. It grunted and moved his head like an owl searching for the source of some strange crux.

Lilith slowly rounded Joe's huge arm and came into full view of the creature. It gasped in surprise and took a step back as if it was shocked by her appearance. He could feel her enter the room and now the creature finally saw her. Its search revealed an answer it was not expecting.

It pulled its arms in and stepped back from the cage wall as if it got caught doing something horrible by its mother. The murderous look instantly was replaced with astonishment. Jack knew right away that Lilith was now the lead interrogator and slowly turned and walked to the table. Lilith saw the creature's reaction as well and tried not to appear as surprised as she was.

She placed her hands behind her and walked up to the cage as if she owned the place. This time she walked right up to the cage wall itself. The creature could easily grab her through the bars. Joe took a step, but Danny immediately held him back. Shooting Danny a stern look, Joe knew Lilith was taking charge, and he needed to stand down. He took a deep breath and stepped back. He was aware that Lilith wanted to show the creature she was not afraid of it. Joe, trying to relax, took a more neutral posture.

When he turned back to the creature, he saw that it was beginning to fidget with his fingers. It looked right at Lilith, not in the least concerned with anyone else. After a few grueling moments, it finally spoke.

"*It's you...*" The thing said speaking German and in a surprisingly pleasant and soft voice.

"Yes it is… and who are you?" Lilith answered, also speaking German to everyone else's surprise. She had no idea she was speaking German but was trying to keep up the appearance of authority. The creature snapped to attention and looked straight forward.

"Augustin Sollner! Unteroffezier Medizin! Neunte Panzerdivision!" the creature yelled enthusiastically.

Lilith shot Joe a look of confusion. Joe then leaned towards Danny and whispered cautiously.

"The thing just said it's a medic in a German unit that was destroyed during World War two… the fuck is going on here?"

"We have no idea. We didn't even think it could speak." Danny whispered back.

Lilith turned to Jack who had grabbed two hypodermic needles filled with tranquilizer just in case. She shook her head and waved Jack back. She somehow put the fear of God in this creature and decided to push the interrogation full-bore without assistance.

"Why are you here Sergeant Sollner?" she asked still speaking German.

"We were ordered here… Fraulein."

"From where?"

"Hell… The Battlefields of Hell. My home now."

Lilith was deeply taken aback by this news. After everything that has happened. She has no doubt he was from the Battlefields of Hell.

"Explain Sergeant."

"Do you not remember Fraulein Lilith? You have been there."

"Remind me. And give details so that my men can understand as well."

Sollner glanced at the other men in the room quickly. He nodded. He turned to Joe and Danny and continued in German.

"We are the Soldiers of the damned. We will fight a war as part of our punishment forever in the Battlefields of Hell. If we refuse to fight, we will be condemned to the machine and tortured for eternity. If we die fighting, we are sentenced to burn in the pit for forty days. It is our punishment for losing the war here on earth."

"Who sent you Sergeant? Why are you here?"

"It was an Archangel! He gave us orders to destroy the world! If we resist, we are sent to the machine forever. The Archangel ripped the veil and mass incarnated us... he then ordered us to war. If we die, we are just incarnated again in hell and go back through the rift."

"Can you take over bodies of the dead?"

"No... of course not. We are damned to fight war forever but that... possession... dishonorable. Those that do that are the lost souls... the sinners. They spilled over from the machine and were not given incarnation. They must roam without form as spirits and steal the bodies of the dead. Dirty souls those ones are. Evil... Perverse!"

"And you're not Sergeant Sollner?"

"I do what I am ordered... I do not want to go to the machine. Nobody would ever want to. The horrors there are a thousand times worse than war. Souls torture and consume other souls forever with no end to the pain and torment. I'm just a simple medic. My job is to keep my men in the fight!" Sollner stated with pride. "See my jaw! I did this. I put it on myself... painful! With the help of my First Sergeant. I even forged it from the pistols of my enemies!" Sollner stated with great enthusiasm moving up to the cage bars for show Lilith.

Lilith glanced at his jaw. The crudely made steel mandible replaced the one the creature at some point in its existence had lost. Upon closer inspection, Lilith noticed that the creature's skin seemed to have been fused to the metal jaw as if it was welded onto his face.

"Who let the souls out, Sergeant?"

"It was an accident I think... The Ark Angel is confident beyond his ability. A few demons escaped as well when I passed through. Evil dark souls those ones are. From deep in the pit... Old souls..." Sollner stated drifting into a daze for a moment.

"The rift... is it still open. Can your soldiers and the others still get through?"

"Yes Fraulein... "

"Is there only one rift?"

"No Fraulein..."

Sollner seemed ashamed as he answered Lilith's questions as if even he didn't want this to happen.

"How do you close the rifts, Sergeant? You are not supposed to be here!"

"I do not know Fraulein... theses are powers beyond me."

Lilith reached in the cage and grabbed Sollner by the back of his head and slammed his head into the bars ruthlessly hard. Black blood began to leak from his forehead. Sollner reacted and reached through the bars grabbing Lilith by her shoulders defensively. Lilith, setting Sollner up, dropped under one of Sollner's arm, pinned it to the cage cross member, yanked hard and broke his arm. Sollner shrieked in pain clawing at the cage like a raged animal.

It happened so quick that the other team member just jumped up and gasped, cursing under their breath in amazement. Danny and Joe covered their mouths trying not to react too much to the sudden violent act. Jack, on the other hand, smirked and nodded his head in approval.

"You sure that's a good idea, Lilith?" Danny asked nervously. Lilith shot him a stern look, jerked up and pulled Sollner's other arm outside the cage ready to break it as well.

"Fraulein, please! I do not know how?" Sollner begged.

"Then who does?!"

Lilith pulled down on Sollner's arm just a bit to take up the slack and let him know what was about to happen.

"Fraulein! No Please...." Sollner stated, but he ended his plea in what sounded like a question.

"Sergeant?! You have a name, don't you! Who is it?"

"Melek!" Sollner yelled out. The name hit Lilith like a baseball bat to the face. She immediately let Sollner's arm go and dropped to a knee. She has heard that name before... Millions of times before. It echoed in her head. She could almost place the moments when she heard it and even said it. But that was a long time ago... Not in this lifetime. At least that is what she thought anyway.

What is going on...? She thought.

"Melek, Fraulein ... Your friend Melek." Sollner stated calmly pulling his mangled arm in and moving slowly and cautiously to the other side of the cage.

"I know you don't remember Lilith. We have fought together. You helped me with my jaw... you helped us all.. augment ourselves. But now you are on the other side. We are enemy's now." Sollner explained as he turned slowly to face Lilith. Lilith quickly stood up and turned, their gaze met.

"I understand... the arm thing. It is ok... It is war...after all." Sollner continued. Lilith didn't know what Sollner was talking about, but for some reason it all made sense. Her dreams made sense now.

"Melek?" She asked.

"Yes... Your friends might know him as Satan." Sollner answered shaking his arm. Lilith's eyes stared at Sollner unblinking. Rage and anger covered her face. She couldn't believe what she was hearing. Satan... her friend? Why? What is happening to the world, she

thought. Everything was crashing around her, and she made no attempt to hide her feelings either. Joe wanted to go to her, but he was having trouble understanding what was happening himself.

In that short time, Sollner's bone had set in his arm and began to heal at an incredibly fast rate. He shook his arm testing its tensile. Confident it was good He turned his attention to Lillith. This time was a bit more confidence.

"You are the only one Melek will ever listen to Lilith... go to him. You'll have to fight, but you can get through the rift. Just you, though. Because you've been before... Also, two more things." Sollner stated with some cockiness.

"One! To kill a Trooper you need to destroy the brain or destroy the body beyond healing!" Sollner added almost shouting.

"And Two?" Lilith asked.

"I know you are sorry for my arm. It is ok. I understand..." Sollner professed. He then straightened up and stared into Lilith's eyes.

"Just like I know you will understand this..." Sollner stated smiling. He paused a second and then took a deep breath. Lilith may have been the only one who noticed right away, but Sollner's veins all over his body filled with whatever filth he was using for blood, and she stepped back.

Sollner sprinted to the other side of the cage slamming his body into the bars. Black blood splattered everywhere. The force bent the bars out almost three inches. He paused as if he got the sense knocked out of him. He Shook his head several times trying to clear his vision. After a second, he then grabbed the bars and by using his legs began pulling the bars apart.

Danny shot to the door and hit a red button mounted to the wall initiating an alarm. Lights and sirens raged suddenly, but it wasn't quick enough. Sollner had Brocken the bars off and was making his way to Jack. With incredible speed, Sollner crossed the room and quickly placed jack in a chock hold. Joe and Danny rushed to Help Jack, but the creature had a good hold of Jack, and they were having difficulty pulling the creature arms off him.

Jack struggled and gasped for air. His lights were about to go out. Joe saw him fading fast and punched Sollner in the face as hard as he could in desperation. Unscathed, Sollner looked Joe in the face and cinched down even harder in protest. Then suddenly, without warning, Sollner's head exploded instantly releasing Jack from the death choke.

Joe and Danny stared at each other, stunned, covered in blood and brain matter as Sollner's body went limp and fell headless backward to the ground. They then turned and saw Lilith standing there with her pistol drawn as smoke escaping from its barrel.

"I said..." Danny began and immediately regretted even opening his mouth.

From behind the two-way glass, Lilith and the others heard the entire observation deck explode in a very boisterous celebration. Lilith looked up and noticed the room filled beyond capacity with various soldiers and personnel. Her team was especially excited. They liked happy endings.

Two hours later...

Lilith stayed out of the way for the most part. The heavily staffed war room was already cluttered with personnel running about and yelling. Funny how much a soldier trains to avoid messes like this but it never seems to come together during a real world mission. The executive officer was going crazy trying to reorganize the room without getting in the way too much. Lilith could tell she hated her job. *Officers... They look so cool in the movies.*

Lilith saw Dave walk in from across the room. He looked up a few steps in and stopped mid-step. It was chaos right now. You could almost smell the fried cranial circuits for everything that was going on. I sighed, shook his head in amazement and then saw Lilith. He made his way across the room as best he could trying not to get in the way. He was carrying two cans of something. Lilith desperately hoped it was beer.

"Soda!?" He said aloud and handed her a can of Heineken stuffed in a US Army Koozie.

"Thank God! You're my hero!" she exclaimed.

"Yeah I know. I'm every woman's hero!" "They just say that because you get them drunk." Lilith teased as she opened her beer.

Dave let her sip the beer a few times. She knew he was there to check on her. Lilith loved Dave like a brother. He was an honest good man. Ready to give his life for his teammates at any time. Lilith loved everyone on her team and couldn't imagine what she would do without them. But Lilith worried that with all the craziness in her life, the incident with Sollner, her freaky past would end up alienating her from the people she loved. She didn't want her team to think she was a freak. Not to forget the fact that she is a Ginger which didn't help either.

She sighed aloud and took a big swig of the beer. She hoped to at least get a small buzz if she could just get it down quick enough.

"I'm assuming the translation is complete on the interview?" Lilith asked coyly.

"Yep!" Dave answered. He paused then turned and faced her.

"I'll admit that I was a little surprised. I mean. It's a lot to chew on, you know?" Dave paused again. He could see Lilith cringe with embarrassment.

"Joe thinks it's cool as shit!" he added just in time.

"What?"

"Yeah. Look I know things are weird, but in the current situation you are about as normal as it gets."

Lilith smirked, but Dave knew it wasn't enough.

"The guys trust you more than they trust anyone else, Lilith. And that's all that matters, right?" Dave stated holding his beer up.

Lilith toasted her drink with his and smiled a real smile.

"I don't know what Sollner was talking about you know?" Lilith finally said.

"It doesn't matter right now. Joe's on the war path, and he's planning an assault on the rift. We will get to the bottom of this for sure." Dave trailed off with an inquisitive but confused look on his face.

"He knew my name... With everything... Everything that is happening. Maybe he's right?" She added.

"What? That you're from Hell?! Bullshit! You're a fucking weirdo, but you're not some demon girl." Dave said turning to her.

"I think he's telling the truth, Dave."   "Lilith that's..." Dave searched for words, but with all the chaos going on in the war room and with the Army from Hell at the gates it was hard to argue.

"The Colonel says there's a are rifts all over the world. The largest that they know of is in Nevada. But there is a small one about fifteen clicks straight out. He wants to make entry with several teams."

"I think we should do what Sollner says." Lilith stood up and slammed the rest of her beer. Dave, shocked that she had finished her beer already, started chugging his. He was having trouble with it though. The cold brew burned the back of his throat. Calmly he coughed and tried to play it off.

"Joe and the Colonel are coming up with a plan to infill the rift thingy. Colonel Montgomery says he has a couple of ODA teams coming in to help."

"Oh No! I'm going alone. Sollner said that I was the only one that could." Lilith stated.

"Are you fucking kidding Lilith. Who knows what bullshit that... thing... Sollner was feeding us." Lilith held her hand up stopping Dave from finishing his thought.

"Is there anymore... 'Soda'?"

"God Damnit Lilith... You're fucking serious!" Dave sounded a little angrier now. He knew the whole situation was crazy. That also includes her going to Hell to see Satan.

"This can't be happening! This whole scenario is complete Bullshit. There is no such thing as Hell and Demons and fucking crazy ass blob giants or scary fucking freak kids! And you are not going to Hell alone, and you are not going to hell to see fucking Satan!" Dave shouted. It was clear that he was in a little bit of disbelief that this Hell war thing even is going on.

It took only a second for the two to realize that everyone in the war room had stopped what they were doing and were just staring at them. Some looked confused, and some even seemed horrified. Dave, clearly embarrassed by his loss of composure, grabbed Lilith's hand and headed for the door.

"Yeah... let's get some... Soda! Damnit!"

A few minutes later Dave and Lilith arrived at the Colonel's briefing room with two fresh beers. There they found the rest of the team, the Colonel, Danny, and Isabella. Everyone stopped what they were doing and looked at Lilith and Dave. For a second there was an uncomfortable null in the activity, but it soon dissipated with Joe's voice.

"There is some Soda in that cooler. Get it while you can because it's all we got." Joe stated.

"Soda. Yeah. I'm on it." Lilith grabbed another cold one and held it up awkwardly.

"Dave come here. I want to show you what we got so far." Joe asked.

Dave looked at Lilith and gave her a nod. A sort of gesture to see that she was feeling good. She nodded back, and Dave headed over to the table.

Lilith looked around curiously. Each room of the asylum looked like a set of a horror movie. It was evident that they chose this building because it could withstand an attack very well, but it made her feel uncomfortable. For a moment, she imagined herself in her loft apartment. The Sun is shining in through her big bay windows and her coffee in hand steaming away. She missed her place. She missed everything that was the world. She knew it would never be the same. Never be like it was.

The rest of the crew were in teams going over the small details and making lists of gear and weapons. Posted on the white board Lilith noted mission brief in about three hours. Lots of time.

Then suddenly, she got scared. Her heart raced and her mind filled with images of her team ripping through Troopers like they were nothing. But the line of invaders never stops. They kept coming and coming. Relentlessly and without end till her team slowly, one by one was killed off.

Not going to happen... She thought.

Lilith walked up to the table. There she saw a map and what looked like a full on frontal assault of three ODA team and various aircraft. She studied it carefully, trying to play the scene in her head. It would work. They could pull it off. But there was one thing wrong. The rift would replenish the ranks within moments. Her fear confirmed the inevitable.

"What is that?" Lilith asked pointing to a large black mass at the river's edge.

"Ummm... Sea Monster?" The colonel answered almost as if he was asking a question.

Surprised but not surprised Lilith processed the situation for a moment. But it was evident, and she knew what to do next.

"Joe..." she said. Joe grunted as he wrote something in his notebook.

"I don't like this. I don't like this at all." She said.

Joe stopped writing and looked at her. "I don't like it either. But we need to find out what is going on here. At the source. We need to see how they are getting here."

"We already know Joe. I need to go. Alone." She stated in a serious voice.

"Like hell you are Lilith. We go in together." Joe said, this time turning towards her.

"We are a team Lilith, and this will work, OK?" "No Joe. You heard Sollner. He was telling the truth!"

"Yeah and he almost killed Jack... all of us if he had the chance." Everyone in the room stopped what they were doing. It was evident that Lilith is going to deal with this now.

"Colonel, I need to go alone. Maybe a discretionary force and a few birds to help me infiltrate. Sollner knew me for whatever reason. If we assault the rift, the team isn't going to make it. They're all going to die for nothing!"

"We don't know that. Three ODA teams and support aircraft will decimate this area like it never existed. Look for yourself. There may be some casualties..." The colonel stopped abruptly when Lilith drew her pistol out of her thigh holster and held it to her side.

"What are you going to do Lilith? Shoot one of us?" The Colonel asked sarcastically. Lilith would never hurt any of her friends or anyone in the room. But she was scared. Joe dropped his notebook and pen and started rubbing his face with his palms.

"Joe this isn't going to work, and I think even you are starting to realize this. Either you help me, or you don't. And if anyone dares grab me I won't hesitate to scar your pretty little faces or give you a nice leg wound."

Everyone in the room put up their hands letting her know they were not interested. This was one of those freaky Lilith moments. They listened before, and they all survived. Still, the room became tense as if mommy and daddy were arguing about cheating or drinking. Best to stay out of it, everyone thought. Nobody was too sure Lilith wouldn't shoot them. Who knew. She might if she thought she was saving them.

"Lilith what are you doing?" the Colonel asked.

"If I go alone… right now. My team will not die for shits and giggles."

"Lilith think about what you are doing. This is treason."

"I would die for my friends…" those words drove deep into her heart. For an instant, clarity poured over her. Joe saw it first and then the rest of the team as well.

"Lilith…" Joe asked calmly.

Lilith finished her beer in a single gulp. Joe thought this would be a good time to jump her and get her gun but deep inside he knew she was right. She put the beer down and looked at Joe in the eye. She was on edge, focused and without a word she walked to the door with her gun to her side and left.

"Fuck!" Joe yelled slamming his fist on the table.

"Stop her Damnit!" the Colonel shouted.

"Like that's going to happen. She'll shoot us for sure and to be honest; I could use a good day or two in the hospital just chilling." Markus stated as he grabbed his gear and left. The rest of Joe's team to include Joe did the same.

"Where is everyone going?"

"To the Helo Pad. Lilith needs air support." Joe stated.

The colonel just stood there rubbing his face wondering what to do. Jack walked up to him and put his hand on his shoulder.

"I know you think she's crazy. But you have to trust her. She… She just knows things. It's hard to explain. Plus we will get to see what the rift is all about." Jack stated with a smile on his face.

"This is total bullshit… you know that right?" The Colonel shouted defiantly

"Yep… but it always works."

Lilith sprinted to the to the ready room and grabbed her gear and then raced to the back window and jumped out. They were on the second floor, but the jump down seemed effortless and gracefully. With the warm night air blowing in her face, she headed for the gate.

The Colonel and Jack made it to the war room and ran inside.

"Where is she?" The Colonel asked loudly.

"Where is who?" The young executive officer asked. Just then a call came over the security net about a woman with a gun trying to get out.

"Let her out! Let her out!" Jack shouted, and that radio operator then looked at the colonel.

"Let her out! Quick!"

The radio operator called over the net and advised the security team to stand down.

Lilith had two handguns up pointed at the two security gate guards as they held their ground at the front gate. The guards held up their rifles blocking the gates but lowered them once they got the word from the war room.

Lilith, however, kept her guns up.

"You're crazy lady going out there alone…" One guard stated as she passed by.

"Yeah… I got that feeling too." She said as she passed the gate and began running down the road. Not far from the gate she came across several fortified positions occupied by a miss match of armed forces and police. Mixed in with the fortifications were some Tank fortifications as well. But the tank fortifications seemed almost too large. The Soldiers and Police had been there for a while by the looks of it. But without a word, everyone watched curiously as Lilith climbed over a berm and headed off into the night.

Lilith, now in no-mans-land, quickly got low and looked for good cover. She was on her own and support will be limited at best. Staying low and quiet, Lilith moved up to a position just passed the line and behind a small pile of brick. There she grabbed her radio, turned it on, and secured the throat mic and earpiecc to her head. Once the radio cycled through its initial testing, she made a commo check with the war room.

"War Room this is Slaughter commo check."

The colonel looked at Jack with a stunned look on his face.

"This is really going to happen isn't it?" he asked.

"Yep!" Jack replied.

The radio operator completed the radio check with a confused look on his face.

"Sir, who am I talking to?" The Operator asked.

"Just go with it son!" The colonel blurted out, obviously annoyed.

The colonel turned to Jack with a concerned look on his face.

"Slaughter?" He asked.

"Yeah, it's uh... Kinda how we met her."

"No Shit?" The colonel responded not too impressed with the use of the word.

"I know what you are thinking Colonel, but this one is different."

"Yeah?! Well, let's hope she is because this whole fucked up thing is definitely like the 'End of the World' shit you know!?"

"She is going to ask for support. We need those Aircraft ready. Anything you got."

"In the Air or on stand by?"

"Stand by... she will call it in when she wants them in the Air." Jack stated.

"Response time?" He asked

"She will need three minutes, in the air, two minutes to time on target... No more."

"God Damn it!" The colonel cursed. That was like the perfect storm that would be almost impossible to coordinate.

"Her run time is about six to six and a half minutes a mile... times fifteen kilometers... we have say sixty minutes' minimum to plan and stage." Jack said.

The Colonel took a deep breath, and then turned to everyone in the War Room. He paused as if he was still struggling the idea. Everyone sat there in high suspense waiting for orders. Then with a quick look at Jack, the Colonel did what he was designed to do... he gave orders.

Lilith put her armor on and loaded minimal equipment in her pack and strapped it tight as to not make any noise when she ran. She then put the pack on her back, check that her rifle and pistol were loaded, and headed across no-mans-land or what was left of Orell Kentucky.

Constant maneuvering and fighting between armor and infantry has destroyed most of the town but provided plenty of cover and concealment for Lilith. When she studied the map in the conference room, she made a mental note as to where everything was. To her West was a river, east were mountains and some sparse living domiciles, and to her south was another small river that would take her to the rift.

Lilith sprinted from cover position to cover position quickly, only taking enough time to scan the area with her night scope as needed. The town was leveled, and scanning was easy enough. The fighting here was fierce and devastating. But something was wrong.

Where are the bodies? She thought.

Blood and gear scattered about the various fighting positions, but not a single body could be found. Or at least whole bodies. Small bits here and there of meat or bone but nothing bigger than a hand. In some areas, it looked as if the bodies were dragged off. Lilith noticed the blood trails and drag marks all lead to the west. Something was dragging all the bodies away and taking them to the river.

Lilith remembered the words from the Colonel. She could hear them in her head echoing. Chills shot up her spine.

Sea Monster?

"What the Fuck...?"

Just then she heard voices and took cover. Peeking over a car hood, Lilith could see a five-man patrol of Incarnated Troopers moving in a wedge formation about a hundred meters away. She pondered if she should engage them or not. She decided to avoid them and silently slid into the garage of a mechanics shop.

From inside she raised her weapon and peered through the scope. The green hues blazed bright making it difficult to see. Cursing under her breath, she adjusted the brightness.

Once satisfied, she studied her targets carefully. All but one carried large automatic weapons. Engaging them didn't seem like such a good idea after all. She lowered her weapon and looked off to the side. There, not far from her, laying in a puddle of blood was a small teddy bear. It looked a little weathered, and Lilith assumed it was someone's... some child's beloved toy bear.

Sorrow filled her heart but was quickly replaced with rage. It swelled up inside her lungs like a disease. No way is she just going to let this pass and reached in a pouch in from her belt. Lilith pulled out a small range finder and targeted the troopers. She noted their distance and direction to which she committed to memory. She then glanced at her Suunto watch and wrote down her ten-digit grid location. That would place her within five meters of her exact location.

Her efforts were suddenly interrupted by a surge in the ground around her. Followed by a powerfully low and deep-toned moan. It was as if the planet just sighed. The sound reverberated deep through her body making it difficult to breathe. She froze instantly, unsure what to do.

Sea Monster?

The troopers immediately stopped and pulled into a tighter formation providing security from all sides. They yelled at each other and pointed their weapons frantically searching for a target. Something spooked them, and Lilith only imagined that is must have been the thing that made the incredible noise. Whatever it was it sounded as if it was the size of a city block. Her heart pounded in her chest as she pushed closer into a panic.

But there was another pulse that she couldn't place. It was strange as if her heart had a third heartbeat. Just then the hairs her arms and the back of her neck stood up. She slowly placed her palm on the ground and closed her eyes. There she could feel the slow thrumping of the creature's heart. Steady and powerful. She could even feel the blood flow through its veins as if thousands of gallons of water flowed under her. She was right on top of whatever it was.

"Holy shit!" She cursed aloud.

To her amazement, Lilith could see the heartbeat of the unknown creature in the puddles of blood around her.

But everything came back into focus as she glanced at the Teddy Bear again.

"War Room this is Slaughter request fire mission, over."

Jack heard Lilith's voice come over the radio and immediately stood up straight.

"Oh! Here we go!"

"Send your fire mission Slaughter, over." The radio operator called over the radio.

"Polar, squad size troops in the open, grid 34USB4764539143, 110 meters at 125 degrees. Danger close. I authenticate November Yankee, Fire for effect, over!"

"This is Fire Control I authenticate Papa. Battery ready!" The artillery commander came over the radio letting everyone on the net know they were ready. The radio operator turned and looked at Jack and the Colonel who both just stared back at him.

"You going to fucking send it guy?!" The Colonel finally spoke up.

The radio operator, who suddenly felt stupid, clicked on the mic.

"Roger! Inbound!"

Lilith moved up to a large piece of concrete and leveled her weapon. In the distance, she could hear the thumping of the artillery cannons sending out about twenty round.

Damn! These guys don't fuck around. She thought.

The point man, who heard the distant thumping as well, put a hand up halting the squad.

Too late fucker!

Lilith pulled the trigger on her AR15 and shot the point man in the head. Several of the squad members began yelling and firing their weapons at an unknown target. But their efforts would be short lived. Just as Lilith stated, it was too late.

A hellfire of artillery rounds began exploding all around the squad in a relentless barrage of death and destruction. Debris and shrapnel shot over Lilith's position as she crouched down behind her cover cursing aloud. Best guess she counted twenty-five rounds. No wonder they can't get through this valley.

As soon as the volley of artillery ended its assault on the enemy squad, Lilith jumped up immediately and scanned for survivors. After a moment, she noticed nothing moving. Not that she thought anything could have survived such a massive hail of artillery, but she wanted to be sure.

"Fire Contol, this is Slaughter, target destroyed. Stand by, out." Lilith commanded over the radio and immediately started moving south.

Just to her left, she noticed a primer black 1969 Coronet. The car was not in pristine condition but had some impressive modifications. Not to mention it looked mean as all hell. Lilith thought that if things were different, she might have bought the damn thing and fixed it up. Brushing the thought of a joyride aside, Lilith continued to head south. Her movements were calculated, carefully, methodically and quickly.

"Sir we may have a problem." A Staff Sergeant leaned over to the Colonel trying to keep quiet.

"What do you got son? It's not like we don't have enough problems." The colonel responded.

"I can't get in contact with several O.P. positions north of our location. It is unlikely both of their radios went down at the same time, Sir."

"Tracking. Send some drones. I want to know what happened to them immediately Staff. We are in a pickle right now with this Lilith girl. I don't want to leave her in the middle of a shit storm unless I have to. Understand? Give me some good intel!"

The Colonel tried to sound firm but not panicked. Jack knew the news of the destroyed observation posts is a bad sign and advised Joe on their internal network. Then for a moment Jack and the Colonel shared a disturbing glance. The shit was about to go down in a bad way.

It didn't take long for Lilith to maneuver through the devastated town and find the staging line for the Incarnated troopers. They didn't keep their positions a secret and Lilith was taken aback as to just how enormous the line was.

From inside a large artillery crater, she made notes on the line. Tanks, entrenched in fighting positions made up most of the line. Hiding in these fighting positions with just their massive turrets exposed were some of the biggest tanks Lilith has ever seen. She recognized some of the Tanks as the old Panzer Tanks, but these tanks were highly modified. Some even sported twin cannon turrets and almost twice their original size. It was no wonder they made such large tank fortifications back at the asylum.

The sound of tanks idling was almost deafening, and her eyes burned from black smoke and embers churned out of their exhaust systems. I looked as if each tank sported two tiny erupting volcanoes. Exhaust could even be seen escaping out of the hatches and viewports well. Stealing a tank was definitely out of the question. She wasn't sure how the tankers lived through such toxic fumes, but she was sure no human could. Still, Lilith was in awe. She could only imagine the devastation these monstrosities could generate.

In-between the tank positions the Troopers built some rather remarkable fighting position with large automatic weapons system surrounded by a rather imposing cover.

But here they all waited to be launched against their enemy. As of right now they stood staged as what could only be Incarnated Sergeants and Commanders walking around shouting and yelling.

She tried hard to ignore the fact that this army came from hell and their mangled bodies were the incarnated souls of the dead Nazi and German Soldiers. The thought was inconceivable not two days before.

Lilith imagined what life would be like once this

enemy is defeated. Or at least if they are defeated. Religious wars were inevitable. Maybe even some race wars as well. It would be a shit storm nonetheless.

Lilith shook off the thought and looked for a way across the seemingly impenetrable line. After a few moments, she realized that the trooper line mine-aswell be a river of lava. There was no way, though.

"War room this is Lilith." She whispered in the mic.

"Go ahead Lilith."

"Sending you some pictures of the line via SipperNet, break." She paused.

"Four in all, over."

"Roger, FYI. Your team is on standby. Four Mini birds. Four Warthogs are on prep. Ready in forty minutes, over. Out."

"Roger, out."

Lilith took several pictures of the line to include equipment and loaded them in her portable Blue Force Tracker and sent them to the war room. The front-line Intel would help later if they decided to advance. However, she still needed to get to the other side.

Then suddenly Lilith had an idea. She then took out a pad and paper, ranged the staging area and her position and wrote it down. She then headed back to the automotive station.

"Predator this is Slaughter. Get the birds in the air and stand by."

"Slaughter this is Predator, five mikes out! Break! We need to hurry. There's something wrong back at base. Over!" Joe responded through the radio.

"Shit!" Lilith cursed hoping she doesn't lose her air support.

Lilith made it back to the old Coronet and popped the hood. Inside she found a huge Hemi 440 accompanied with twin 88mm turbos.

"Fuck yeah!" Lilith whispered and just as she hoped. The Coronet looked like it was built for racing and she was sure this car was a winner too. The inside was set up with a roll cage and a fire extinguisher system. All she needed to do was start it. After placing the battery cable back on the battery, she jumped inside. To her surprise, the thing was ready to go. She unlocked the fuel and hit the push start.

The car rocked to life as if it had been waiting forever for this moment. The straight pipes would make communication with War Room problematic, nonetheless. Lilith thought she was sure she was going to lose at least a little hearing out of this mission. Not caring about that too much right now she strapped in and waited for the oil pressure to raise up. Once the oil pressure was good to go, she revved the motor. The Coronet exhaust was viscously loud and the twin turbo deafening.

Suddenly, Lilith saw something move to her right. She drew her weapon and aimed out the window. To her horror, she saw one of the mangled bodies of the squad of troopers she destroyed earlier being dragged across the ground by a large black tentacle. This would explain why the town lacked bodies. Then suddenly the very tip of another black tentacle peeked over the edge of the door on the passenger side. Whatever it was out there, it has found her.

"Shit!" Lilith shrieked and nailed the throttle. The Coronet thundered in response as she shot into the debris-ridden street like she just robbed a liquor store. The whine of the twin turbos screamed in her ears to the point that is was almost painful. But nothing compared to the thunder of an open piped 440 cubic in Hemi.

There's no fucking way they won't hear me coming! She thought. She needed a distraction, and she needed it quick.

"Predator this is Slaughter, request air support on my mark, over." She yelled into the mic as loud and clear as she could over the roaring monster under her hood.

"Roger Slaughter, ID your position!"   Lilith pulled a small IR strobe a pouch on her vest and turned it on. She then attached the strobe to the roof of the vehicle with the use the attached magnet.

"IR strobe on a fast mover, over."
Joe and the crew popped over the ridge line flying nap of the earth and as fast as the Black Hawks could go. Alongside the team was to Little birds and two more Cobras. Everyone noted the only strobing object in their field of vision and noted it as a friendly.

"Got it, stand by!"

Stuffed in the back of an OH58D Surveillance Helicopter as it peeked its monstrous camera system over a hilltop sat Dave. Dave wished he was there with the team but knew he was the best for surveillance and counter-surveillance operations. In the three screens showing him thermal and night vision images sat the Incarnated Troopers line. It was thick, and he had a hard time figuring out where to start.

"Predator this is Creeper, this line is massive, what the fuck? Over!"

"Creeper from what I can see just start killing shit ok? She's almost to the line!" Joe responded cursing under his breath.

The pilot turned to Joe.

"Is she Fucking crazy man!" the pilot asked.
"Only if she doesn't make it! No focus bro!" Joe said.

Dave pointed two inferred lasers on the two tanks in the front of the line and then tapped his mic. Trying to stay calm he called for fire support from the Cobras.

"umm...Roger. Break, Apache One and Two, Target Lazed. Engage! Engage! Engage!"

The two Cobra helicopters peeled off and raised up just high enough to target the tanks and not expose themselves in the process. The Cobras weapons guy armed their missiles systems and called back their disposition to the pilot. A loud tone came on as the targeting system tried in vain to lock onto the tank, but the distance and the flight speed made it difficult.

Lilith, driving just a little too fast, pulled out her notebook and opened a channel.

"Fire Control this is Slaughter, Polar, Armor entrenched, grid 34GF4563940212, 305 meters at 225 degrees. Danger close. Request Smoke! Over!"

"Slaughter this is Fire Control, Battery ready!" The Battery Commander responded.

"Battery Commander this is War Room! Send it!"

Lilith slowed the vehicle down to a slow crawl. The troopers spotted her and ran to their predetermined fighting position as the tanks revved their motors and began rotating their guns in her directions.

"Five seconds out!" Joe sounded as the helicopters began their attack run.

Lilith waited... And waited... It was only seconds, but it seemed like hours. Then, there it was!

Four Maverick missiles sent from the Cobra shot over her car blasting her with rocket fire and exhaust just as the smoke rounds began impacting. Twenty-five multi-colored smoke shells encased the entire grid square with smoke. Four massive explosions lit up the area as the Maverick turned the massively armored tanks into billowing mounds of fire and debris.

Lilith nailed the gas and started her run as Joe and the team rounded the corner spraying the entire area with minigun and cannon fire. Tracer rounds blasted by Lilith but she didn't worry. She knew that her team wouldn't hit her. They were too good.

"Fire Control this is Slaughter, Repeat fire mission with WP followed by HEAT! Fire for effect!"

Lilith scanned the line and saw a soft spot that

would give her the edge that she needed. She slammed the shifter back downshifting hard and nailed the gas. The engine roared, and the turbo's screamed. Her body pressed against the seat as the Cornet launched forward. Tracer rounds blasted by in both directions as friendly fire, and enemy fire started closing in on her. Twenty-millimeter rounds from the Cobras and the Incarnated Troopers AntiTank rifles started finding the hull of her car. Showers of sparks and shrapnel blasted the inside of the Coronet burning her skin and testing her armor.

Then, just as she reached the line, white phosphorous round exploded overhead blasting brilliant blossoms of burning death across the battlefield. Her only mission now was to get past the line and out of the way of the white phosphorous without dying in the process. The burning chemical would melt through the thin layer of steel of the Coronet like it was paper. Shifting and gunning the motor the twin turbos screamed as she launched her vehicle up a pile of dirt used to entrench the now burning tank positions. With a massive lurch, the car went weightless as it sailed through the air. The only thing now was to land without rolling or damaging the vehicle too much. But that never seems to work out too well. Time slowed to a crawl.

Lilith was amazed as to how bright the white phosphorous burned. The entire area lit up as if the sun exploded. She gasped in awe as she looked around. The scene was incredible. Tracers, missiles, cannon fire, artillery blasted the area with such ferocity and tenacity that it would be any body's wonder if anything could survive. But the view was short lived.

The Coronet hit the ground almost nose first and immediately went into a roll. Lilith didn't remember much about the landing. The only thing she remembered is a high pitched ringing and a fleeting dream of her back at her loft apartment kitchen. She was sipping coffee, but this time she wasn't alone. A man was with her.

He was maybe middle aged and incredibly handsome, Dirty blonde and piercing amber eyes so powerful that they almost glowed. Or did they glow? He looked at Lilith and smiled a perfect smile as if he was amused at something Lilith said. Then, without a word, he held up his hand and snapped his finger.

Pain…! Pain shot through her body. Lilith opened her eyes grunting. Her face was wet with blood. She could smell it.

Fuck! That was dumb! She thought then realizing she landed upside down. Blood flowed profusely from her face as she gathered up the metallic liquid from her throat and spit it out.

This doesn't help either.

Then a flickering ball of burning mass landed just outside her car. She squinted and tried to focus, but the mass was so bright and made her dizzy. She realized what it was. It was the White phosphorous cloud, and it was descending all around her.

"Shit!" she yelled as several rounds impacted her car making it heave back and forth. She scrambled for the harness lock and unbuckled herself. She instantly slammed into the roof hard making her dizzy again. Lilith then scrambled out of the car in a panic.

She struggled to get to her feet and took a second to orient herself. Again, tracer fire crisscrossed the battlefield from all directions as the multicolored clouds of smoke flickered brightly from artillery and rocket fire.

Bringing her weapon to bear, she painfully sprinted behind the enemy lines and out of the white phosphorous cloud.

Several troopers attempted to engage Lilith but were killed off with several well-placed shots to the head. She never slowed her movement and sustained a full sprint while shooting.

Troopers began screaming all around her as the phosphorous cloud engulfed them. Panic welled up, and she forced her legs to move even faster. Blood in her eyes clouded her vision, and her lungs burned with smoke and heat from the battlefield. Lilith stopped wasting time shooting troopers and palmed her weapon to her chest out of instinct. But her surge didn't last long. She could feel the heat on the back of her neck.

She wasn't going to make it.

Like a gift from the gods Lilith ran into a giant mud puddle, and painfully body slammed into it. She rolled and rolled hoping the mud will extinguish the burning phosphorous ambers. She could hear the screams of troopers all around her burning to death. After a few moments, the phosphorous onslaught ceased.

Lilith rolled to her back covered head to toe in a thick layer of mud and chuckled.

"I fucking made it!" she yelled gleefully as she lifted her head up and looked around. But her celebration was short lived. It was something she said earlier that made the pit of her stomach fill with despair. She remembered that she ordered Fire Control to launch HEAT rounds after the white phosphorous round. So, she wasn't out of the woods yet.

Lilith jumped up and got to her feet quickly. Unfortunately, three other Troopers found the magic mud puddle and jumped to their feet as well. Although shocked, Lillith drew her pistol and engaged her targets. Everything was good for the first two troopers. They never got a shot off before she shot them in the head. The third, however, did get a shot off and nailed Lilith in and thigh just before she got him in the head. She dropped to a knee reeling in pain.

For an instant, she wasn't sure, but she thought that she could hear the twenty-five High Explosive round falling onto her position. Even over the chaos of the incredible firefight still in full swing, she could swear she heard them.

Automatic gunfire began blasting all around her splashing mud into her face. She quickly got to her feet still in incredible pain and sprinted off to the south.

For a second there was silence as if everyone realized what was about to happen and took their last 'oh shit' breath. Then the rounds hit.

Lilith heard when the first round hit. Everything else consisted of a high-pitched ringing sound. Even her vision blurred like she was dreaming. She stumbled, trying to stay on her feet and outrun the onslaught. Shockwave after shockwave blasted her body, but she kept to her feet and ended up in slamming against a wall in a makeshift bunker.

There she was met by several troopers somewhat shocked that she made it that far. She raised her weapon praying that it still functioned and doubled tapped two troops with blinding speed and accuracy. She then bolted forward and kicked one trooper in the chest, pulled out her handgun and shot him in the face before he could react. Two more Troopers ran in the bunker with heavy weapons but only got a few rounds off before Lilith shot them both in the head. She quickly reloaded both weapons and ran out of the bunker.

Laying fire, she slowly moved to where the rift should be by what she saw on the map. It didn't take long and neither did it need an identification. It was evident where the rift was.

Lilith, at a disadvantage, sprinted uphill to the top of the Incarnated Army's battlements taking head shots at whoever dared peek over. Reaching the top, she jumped into a deep trench embattlement that mazed in and around other tank emplacements. Lilith sprinted down the trench firing head shots along the way. She then came to a Tank emplacement and ran up on its turret.

There Lilith pulled off her IR strobe from her vest and placed it on the top of the tank's hatch. Rounds from enemy gunfire started impacting the tank hull showering sparks in all directions as she jumped off and back into the trenches.

She kicked a trooper there in the chest launching him back and then shot him in the face twice with her rifle. She then spun around and killed two more Troopers coming around the corner. Without hesitation, she darted down the trench shooting anything that moved.

"Creeper this is Slaughter. Target my strobe hurry! Break!"

Lilith yelled as she dropped four more troopers before continuing. Rounds were coming in all directions now, and she was having trouble running through the trenches.

"Predator this is Slaughter! Strafe fire the line at the marked tanks and hurry!"

"Roger Slaughter, 1 Mike! Over!" Joe acknowledged

"Get the Fuck over there buy like time Now!" Joe shouted at the pilot as the all four helicopters leaned in and charged the battlefield. Now that the artillery barrage has ended the helicopter slowly moved in over the battlefield desperately trying to reach Lilith and provide her with some much-needed air support.

"Slaughter this is Tusk 1 and 2 approaching you three o'clock, subsonic at two hundred feet. Mark your position for a clean sweep." The A10 Warthog pilot called over the radio as the two aircraft prepared their weapons systems.

But Lilith was a little busy at the moment. A trooper jumped from the top of the trench and slapped her weapon from her hands. It didn't go far since it was attached to her vest, but it made killing the trooper more difficult. It punched her twice in the face knocking her back slamming her into the trench wall. The Trooper then grabbed her by the throat. Instinctively she placed the heel of her right foot in the waist crease of the trooper and lifted herself up. She then twisted around and wrapped her left leg over his head and around his neck so that the back of her knee was over his larynx. With all her might she jerked back breaking its arm as the two fell to the ground. With the trooper growing in pain as Lilith hit the button on her throat mic.

"Tracer Rounds!" was all she could get out and started firing rounds straight up in the air just as three more troopers jumped over. Not wasting time she fired round after round keeping the Troopers at bay as much as she could.

"On target! On Deck! 10 seconds!" She heard over the radio. Just then the Cobras missiles impacted the Tank she marked sending the shock wave through the trenches like a tidal wave reaching her position in microseconds hurling the troopers over her and her broken armed friend.

Lilith dropped her rifle and drew her pistol firing four rounds into the unarmored armpit of the opponent. She then lifted her left leg and fire one round directly in the troopers gasping mouth.

Jumping to her feet, she finished off the three other Troopers with two quick headshots each. Just as she reloaded, she could hear the A10's twenty-millimeter rotary cannons belching rounds. Lilith took cover, and the two Aircraft in tight formation laid exploding rounds down the line on both sides of the trenches. Dirt and debris flew through the air all about her almost burying her. Then, not a half a second later the A10's flew by just feet off the ground.

"Moving!" Lilith shouted into her mic, jumping to her feet. She sprinted up the now destroyed trench walls and leveled her weapon. Lilith then grabbed a lanyard with three chem lights and broke their casing activating them. She then put the lanyard around her neck and threw the chem lights to her back so that Joe and the others could see her.

"Predator on me!"

"Roger, two hundred meters to your six!" Joe returned.

Lilith could now see the rift through the darkness. It was about three hundred meters away, carved into a solid rock cliff wall. It wasn't what she thought it would look like. It just looked like a cave entrance. The entrance was about twenty meters high and a couple of hundred meters wide. Smoke and exhaust billowed out from the top of it while troopers and tanks rolled out by the dozens.

It was evident now where the rift is. No need for markers. Lilith started her run to the entrance. Her timing has to be perfect.

"Tusk 1 and 2, start drilling the entrance. Predator, carve me a path over here."

The A10 started the approach launching twenty-millimeter cannon rounds into the cave just over Lilith's head while the helicopters laid massive suppressive fire to her left and right. The amount of ammunition and tracer round lite the entire grid in a brilliant red aurora with fiery explosions, showers of sparks, and burning embers blasted in all directions. Lilith killed anything that was unlucky enough to show itself in front of her as she carved her way to the cave entrance.

Lilith conducted a reload with her last magazine as tracer rounds blasted by her from both the front and the rear. Giving faith a try, Lilith put her head down and sprinted as fast as she could go into the cave entrance closest to the southern side. Unfortunately, her plan was not a very good one.

Once inside a tank round slammed into the wall next to her and knocked her off her feet. She flew through the air and landed on her shoulder. Quickly, she got to her feet and sprinted deeper in the cave. But with a quick glance over her shoulder, her heart dropped and time seemed to slow to a crawl.

Hundreds of tanks and thousands of troopers sat ready to exit the cave entrance as if they were staged there on purpose. The A10's were destroying targets, but it was only denting the overall numbers of Armor and Troopers.

The Incarnated Troopers were purposely hiding their numbers. They were going to attack the

Sanitarium by flooding the battlefield with tanks and infantry. It would be a slaughter.

The few Troopers close to her began an onslaught of rifle and cannon fire. To stay ahead of the firestorm she sprinted as fast as she could to the nearest cover position. Cannon rounds and high powered automatic rifle fire slammed into the cave wall producing a distinctive supersonic popping sound. Shrapnel and small arms fire found her little body though as she dove behind a giant boulder. Tumbling to a stop, she winced in pain as she struggled to crawl away.

Suddenly the tanks large diesel motors began to fire up one by one until the cave filled with a thunderous roar. No more than a moment later tank rounds hammered the large rock Lilith was using for cover, slowly eat away at the rock till it was just a shadow of what it was. The concussion of the rounds pushed Lilith to almost unconsciousness. As if by instinct alone, she painfully and desperately crawling away. Lilith eventually hid inside a horizontal crack in the wall, pushing herself in as far as she could go leaving a massive blood trail behind her.

There was barely enough room for her and her gear, but she managed to slide in sideways a few meters. Dread started to creep into her mind.

"Fuck!" She called out as the tank rounds stopped impacting the wall. She lay there on her belly trying to breathe but was having difficulty with such little space. She closed her eyes.

What have you done Lilith! She thought to herself. Just then dread turned into panic.

Voices and footsteps closed in to where she entered the crack in the wall. Lilith tried to move further into the crack, but her armored chest rig prevented her. Pulling the cord awkwardly out of its anchor, Lilith was able to detach the large portions of the plate carrier from one and other. Once free, she was able to weasel her way out. Just in time too.

Automatic weapons fire from several rifles began striking the crevis where Lilith entered. They were here, and they were pissed. With a little trouble, she grabbed her pistol and moved further back from the entrance. The crack moved downward slightly. The troopers made it to the hollow Lilith hide in and fired their weapons randomly in the crevis. Lilith closed her eyes, rocks chips and shrapnel blasted her face and body. She anticipated the bullet strike, but it never came.

Lilith pushed further back desperately trying to find a way out. Space closed in around her, and she could feel the tracked vehicles rolling out of the rift just a few hundred meters away through the stone slabs compressing her. More yelling and automatic gunfire came from the crevis entrance again pushing her further back.

"Predator this is Slaughter, Over!" She yelled into the mic, but there was no answer. The battle still waged outside, though. She could still hear the gunfire from the miniguns. But she was trapped now. There was not much else to do.

Just then Lilith heard one of the Troopers ask for a grenade. Panicking she looked around for an escape, but there wasn't one. The space was so small, she couldn't even turn her head around and since she was so far in it was too dark to see anything anyway. The rock slabs were crushing her making it difficult to breathe. She needed to move and move now, or she would pass out.

In a panic, Lilith mustered all her strength and pushed back further and further. Suddenly her foot felt space behind her just as the Troopers tossed the grenade.

Scurrying, she pushed back into the crevis and then found herself hanging from a cliff wall. Dangling from a rock face unsure of how far it was to the ground below her and unable to see in the dark, she tossed her pistol in hopes of finding the bottom. But there was nothing. She heard nothing.

"Shit!" She gasped. Then she heard the wooden handled grenade clanking down the crack towards her. She needed to get away from it, but she had no place to go.

The grenade went off, and the shock wave blasted Lilith into the dark unknown. She flailed her hands and feet in an attempt to grab anything around her, but there was nothing. She then spun around and placed her hands in front of her thinking she was about to hit the ground but again... nothing. Thirty seconds into her fall she reached terminal velocity. The air rushed by her ears with defining sound but she could

still hear her panicking heart. A minute went passed...
still nothing. Two minutes passed. No ground. No walls.
No water. No nothing. Just emptiness.

After a few moments, she spun around onto
her back and pulled out a Night Vision Reflex Sight and
switched it on. She then put it to her eye as best she
could and looked around. It took a second to realize
what she was looking at but once it set in her heart
sank.

She was falling in a massive vertical cave. It was
irregular in shape with absolutely no bottom. From wall
to wall must have been at least fifteen hundred meters
or so with jagged cliff walls. Only an experienced rock
climber would be able to scale these wall.

Lilith tried several times to maneuver to the
rock walls hoping to find a way to stop falling. Every
second she fell was at least an hour hike up. Lilith was
desperate and willing to do anything. But every time
she tried she couldn't get close enough. She rolled to
her back trying to relax. At least fifteen minutes went
by, and her situation became bleak. It would take days
to climb the walls, and she was becoming exhausted
just falling. She tried again. And again. And again.
Nothing.

An hour went by, and she peered through the
Night Vision again. To her surprise, she saw giant alien
sculptures carved into the cave wall. Sculptures of faces
of beings that were not only unidentifiable but also
terrifying. Lilith fell past several of these sculptures.
Each different than the last but just as horrifying.

Mass Incarnate

A few times she could see what looked like cave dwellings. Dark unknown figures milled about far away with their silhouettes backlit by small bonfires. She shouted for help, but none came. She wasn't even sure if she wanted help from whoever it was that lived there.   Four hours later her body began to ache badly. Her head hurt, and her eyes became dry and made it difficult to see anything. Dizzy she tried to look through the night vision again. But to no avail. The batteries were dead. She took that as a sign. She was exhausted. In pain. Barely able to stay conscious.

She didn't want to pass out and desperately tried to stay awake. She screamed and slapped herself, but the feeling to just let go was too strong.

Lilith what have you done...

Five hours or so later she finally felt it was time. She hurt all over. She was low on blood and exhausted. It was time. She said a little prayer. Not for her but her team. She wanted her team to go on and be happy. She didn't matter. Lilith then thought of Joe and her friends, said goodbye, and let go of consciousness.

…. To be continued.

www.ingramcontent.com/pod-product-compliance
Lightning Source LLC
Chambersburg PA
CBHW031718170626
46808CB00005B/1794